THE MAGDALENE PROPHECY

TREASURE HUNT

SHAMS-TABRIZ

ESTIECHE MEDIA

Brother, Son, Soul
We only ever hunt to know ourselves

CHAPTER 1

*Y*ael stepped lightly, near-dancingly, through the streets of Turin, Italy. Gone was the steeliness that defined her, the armor of the Perfect Warrior. What remained was the perfect embodiment of a virgin inner-skyscape born of grey clouds swept clear.

Her eyes glistened with the sun. A powder blue floral dress swished airily from her hips.

Turin was an architectural wonder. Everywhere she looked, she was transported three and four hundred years back in time to the origin of the ornate, baroque extravagance surrounding her.

As she crossed Via Accademia delle Scienze, she couldn't know that she was about to begin an adventure paved with ill-fitting bricks which could only be signaling caution. A few days earlier, Yael had solved the mystery surrounding the theft of the Magdalene Treasure. There really had been nothing to solve, only to uncover. The theft had occurred a half-century before and ended in disaster when an explosion had destroyed the Treasure.

In the course of her investigation, she'd met Thomas Esti. His property featured a statue that perfectly matched an image used on the ransom envelope's wax seal.

Thomas was a beautiful man. Beautiful, gentle, kind and generous — *Giving*. He was a man unlike any she'd ever known before. Yael was enjoying being with him. Enjoying it a lot. She knew that she was on the cusp of all new possibilities for herself and her life. But such thoughts would have to wait.

Yael was alone on this trip. She'd left Thomas at his home in Maddalena.

"A few errands to run," she'd explained. "I might head over to Turin. Pop in on a friend. Give me a week. Then I'm all yours."

The truth she'd not told Thomas was that she still had a final set of tasks to attend to before she could put her last assignment behind her. She'd just set out to complete them when one loose end had tugged.

Yael's investigation into the theft of the Magdalene Treasure had begun when a ransom demand had been received by Cardinal Panos Sideris at the Vatican. It had ended horrifically when the thieves had been in an accident on their way to the ransom exchange. The Treasure was destroyed and the thieves had been killed — Carlo Rinaldi, a curator at the Vatican Museums, and his mysterious female accomplice.

Yael had taken to thinking of the duo as the likeness of Bonnie and Clyde. It gave her a name for the anonymous woman. She was the Bonnie to Carlo's Clyde. And while Yael's curiosity had really been piqued by Bonnie—curiosity and fascination both—this was not her focus today.

Yael was interested now in identifying whoever had sent the ransom demand almost fifty years after the fact. Who had sent it and perhaps more importantly, why? It was the one anomaly in the otherwise neat conclusion to her investigation, the last loose thread that hadn't been stitched.

Her employer, Ben Saba, had closed the case without any care to that thread. But as Yael saw it, whoever had sent the ransom letter must have had it to send.

So the question became, who had access to Bonnie & Carlo's things? She was quite sure she'd exhausted all the leads the evidence had to yield. Which meant all she was left with were the witnesses from 1973. Anyone whose name had come up in some way in the investigation of the theft.

Decades had passed. Time was against her. But Yael knew she had skills. *Mad skills.* And it was worth exploring.

CHAPTER 2

*Y*ael had moved the ball forward quickly after that. While the files containing the identity of the people she was seeking were in the possession of Special Inspector Francesco Falco in Naxos, Yael did remember the name of Falco's venerable lieutenant, Carmine Vespucci. Unfortunately, an online search of news archives revealed he was long gone. Killed in the line of duty back in the Eighties.

But then the woman with the memorable name came to mind. Marion Moreau. She was the museum staffer who'd reported seeing Carlo leave the Vatican gala early two nights before the theft.

Yael found Moreau online. The woman was the director of the Egyptian Museum. Yael was now in Turin to question her.

Still walking at a bold clip, she entered the building housing the Museo Egizio di Torino. It was an architectural behemoth that took up the bulk of the circumference of a city block. One of its features was a large, rectangular central courtyard.

Inside, Interpol credentials and a brief explanation of her presence quickly passed Yael into the office of the Director who was standing behind her desk with an outstretched arm.

"How exciting! I'm thrilled! So happy to oblige an international police examination. Cold case art burglaries, no less!" Moreau spoke with a smooth French voice rich in timbre despite her age, perhaps richer because of it. She was very chatty which would serve Yael well.

"I'd like to take you back to 1973," Yael said as she sat down. "Carlo Rinaldi."

"Carlo was suspected of stealing an objet d'art. A bronze globe, I believe. I can't imagine what would have made it so worthy of being stolen. I didn't know the piece, so there's not much I can tell you."

"When was the last time you saw him?"

"I remember it well," she sighed as if to call forth a sad memory. "It was at a party held at the Vatican. Carlo was there, but he arrived late. He was preoccupied. Avoided me. It was so unlike him. Something was definitely off.

"We had something going, you know? I was sure that was going to be the night. At least third base, as the Yanks say." A tight smile pushed through her sadness. "The next thing I know he was sneaking out of the room. He didn't even say goodbye. I never saw him again. It was a tough time for me. My broken heart took a long time to mend."

"I'm sorry," said Yael.

"You got my name from the police records, I presume. I didn't enjoy— How do they say it in the movies? Ratting on him to the cops? But they'd brought in a Chief Inspector of the national police. Threats of obstruction and interference were being leveled all over the place.

"Not that I said anything to hurt Carlo. Just the facts. I mean, he did leave early. It was the gala, after all. And Carlo was the life of the party. Always. I wasn't the only one to miss him that night."

Yael took note of the guilt shading Moreau.

"I never found out what happened. And I couldn't believe he was a thief. But then it was obvious.

"Word was he showed up at work on Monday morning, committed the crime and was never seen after that. He just disappeared.

"Time just passed. I suppose I figured he was holed up in jail somewhere."

"Is there anything else you can remember that might be of help?"

"There were rumors that Carlo had been seen with a woman."

"Rumors?"

"Well, all the female employees were rounded up and interrogated for hours. None of the men got that kind of attention. And considering the questions, it was pretty obvious that they were looking for a woman who had no alibi for the gala night. Or the following Monday morning."

"And—?"

"We all did."

"Did anyone see this woman?"

"No. But I know what she looked like."

"How?"

"Carlo had a type."

"She might not have been a love interest," said Yael.

"Well independent of that, I could still tell you what she looked like."

"Go on."

"There was a very specific profile to the people they questioned the hardest. They were all slender women around thirty."

"That's it?"

"Yes."

"Light hair or dark?"

"Uh," she said, trying to recall. Then just shook her head.

"Short or tall?"

"Shorter than Carlo, I suppose."

"How tall was he?"

"He was a giant."

This wasn't as helpful as Moreau might have thought. It left too much undefined. "And Carlo's type?" she asked.

"I just told you. Slender. Not young. Not old."

"Did he have any other noteworthy preference in women? Complexion, hair color, ethnicity? Anything like that?"

"Oh yes! But you're too young to understand how some of us exercised our freedoms back then."

CHAPTER 3

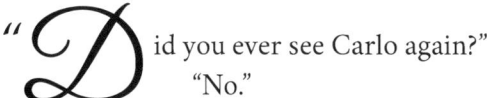

"*D*id you ever see Carlo again?"

"No."

"You didn't hear from him?"

"No. But his name came up about a year later. I was going through some pieces that had been previously catalogued from the Lateran Palace. These were items that hadn't made their way into the Vatican's Historical Museum and hadn't yet been placed anywhere else.

"All of the boxes had labels pasted on them, actually single sheets of paper, that listed their contents. One of the boxes had a label that didn't match the master list I'd been given by the museum director. The box's register had one line missing. It was the line that described a twelfth-century scepter that was a gift to Pope Innocent III, supposed-booty from the fourth Crusade.

"Needless to say, the scepter was gone. I reported my findings, and the Gendarmerie got involved. Chief Cornaz was a bulldog. Unusually so, I think. If I was to guess, he was still reeling from having been out-ranked on Carlo's theft by someone from the Italian State Police back in 1973. Remember, this was the Vatican. And the Vatican isn't Italy. The Italian State Police had no real jurisdiction. But Cornaz had been overruled by someone with Vatican clout. And the result was Carlo had gotten away with whatever this bronze globe was that he'd stolen.

"With my discovery of the missing scepter, Cornaz wasn't about to tolerate a casual investigation. He ordered an inspection of the paper labels from the boxes containing the Lateran pieces. It was discovered that the same typewriter had been used for the box that was supposed to hold the scepter as for the others. It was also the same typewriter used for the director's master list. In other words, the person who had catalogued the contents was also the person who'd stolen the scepter and altered the listing."

"Carlo," said Yael.

Moreau nodded absently. "I shouldn't have been surprised after what happened in '73. As they say, once a thief, always a thief. I guess there was no way around it. He changed the record. He must have taken the scepter."

"Nothing else was missing from the Lateran collection. But because of the cloud that hung over Carlo from before, Cornaz expanded the investigation. A physical inventory was run on everything in the Vatican collection."

"More thefts?"

"Not at first. They didn't actually find anything missing. But Cornaz had a chip on his shoulder. He wasn't about to let anything slip and left no stone unturned. The entire curatorial department was commissioned to inspect every single item in the Vatican collection. You can imagine the insanity."

She caught her breath and looked off into her thoughts. "I don't think I could have imagined the outcome. I didn't believe it at first."

"What did you find?"

"We weren't permitted to talk about it at the time. I'm sure the higher-ups were all concerned about what a huge embarrassment it would be for the Vatican. They had to keep it out of the news." Moreau paused and fixed her eyes on Yael.

"What we found was catastrophic."

CHAPTER 4

"What was catastrophic? What did you find?" Yael pressed.

"Counterfeits. Over thirty objects from the Vatican collection," said Moreau.

"Do you remember what they were?"

"They were all papers. Check with the Vatican Gendarmerie Corps. They'll have the list."

"You said 'papers'?"

"Paintings and scrolls. There was no way to know when exactly the thefts had occurred. Only that they'd stopped when Carlo disappeared."

Yael wasn't satisfied with that conclusion. As she saw it, the thefts could have occurred at any time between the time they'd come into the Vatican Collection and the time the fraud had been discovered in '75. Unless there was a record of verifiable authentications in the interim that would have shrunk the timeline. And even if there had been, how could they be trusted? They could easily have been fudged to conceal the counterfeit nature of the objects in question.

"What happened to the originals?"

"Who knows? The Blackmarket. Unscrupulous private collectors.

They were never removed from the Vatican's inventory books, but that means nothing. It could have been just another tactic to avoid more Church embarrassment. I've seen a lot of that over the years. I don't think the stolen items were ever found."

"Was Carlo an artist?" Yael asked.

"Right, you mean in order to replicate the originals," said Moreau. "That's the odd thing. No. He wasn't. He could barely doodle. I mean, it's a surprise that he chose this as his career. Not to say that he wasn't good at what he did. He was. But he wasn't a conservator-restorer. That would have required exceptional technical skills which he just didn't have.

"Most people don't know that conservators are great artists. They have to be in order to undertake the detailed, painstaking restoration process of aged art. Carlo was more of an art historian. A valuator. And an authenticator. Involved in acquisitions. But there's no way he could have created replicas good enough to pass unnoticed for years at the *Museum of Museums*, let alone any other. No way!"

"Do you have any idea who could have pulled it off?"

"I know exactly who! That vixen. That... that tart I told you about. The one they'd been looking for in '73. I'd bet my life on it."

"Based on what?"

"Carlo had a weakness for women. I'm telling you, she's the one who turned him to the dark side."

These were the words of a woman scorned. Maybe even a blackened pot smearing the kettle. At the same time, what Moreau said did make sense. Carlo's veiled accomplice—Bonnie, as Yael knew her—might very well be the artist who'd produced the counterfeits.

Yael was sure about one thing. Carlo Rinaldi was a criminal mastermind. He'd positioned himself as a reputable curator in arguably the most prestigious museum in the world, all the while literally robbing from Peter!

CHAPTER 5

A short while later, Yael sat alone in the central courtyard of the Egyptian Museum. She rummaged through the satchel she'd seized from Marco Grappone, Cardinal Sideris's secretary, after his death.

She turned her attention to the report which documented all missing and stolen items from the Vatican Museums. As she scanned through it, she could find no record of the thirty-odd counterfeits that had been discovered in '75. She found the notation reporting the stolen scepter but absolutely nothing that would account for the host of other 'papers' Moreau had told her about.

This meant that Cornaz had intentionally kept the thirty other thefts off the official books. It explained why Moreau had been sworn to secrecy. But it didn't explain why Cornaz would have concealed the thefts of the thirty papers in the first place.

Was it, as Moreau had said, to save face for the Vatican? Or was it because Cornaz had still been stinging from being thrown off the case of Magdalene Treasure in '73? Had he been steeped in pride to such excess?

Yael could get to the bottom of this if she could just find Cornaz. She wasn't holding her breath. As Falco himself evidenced, anyone in a position of seniority back then was either in their waning years or already gone.

Yael opened the Interpol search engine she had access to by virtue of the front provided by Ben Saba. After plugging in a series of over-riding passkeys and faltering through a few false starts, Yael hit on a police report of the suspicious death of the Chief of the Vatican Gendarmerie.

Antoine Cornaz had been trekking the wilderness alone at dawn around his family's villa in the Alps when he'd disappeared. The police who'd first found his body thought he'd been shot. A large caliber bullet-hole cut through the singed layers of clothing on his back. But further examination proved the cause of death was electrocution. The investigation fumbled until it was discovered that a freak lightning storm had washed through the mountain pass early that same morning.

That effectively struck down any chance of answers from Cornaz. If only Yael could get her hands on his '75 investigation files. But Tech would be useless in this instance. Files from the Seventies hadn't been digitized. Marco's log of missing and stolen items served as proof of that fact — everything before 1980 had been photocopied from a handwritten logbook. Which meant that she couldn't possibly expect Cornaz' files to be digitized.

And if Yael dared to show up at the Vatican to examine old police records, it would raise questions she wasn't prepared to answer. Not to Sideris. Certainly not to Ben. What was she to do? Without auditing the Gendarmerie's investigation files from 1975, how would she know if any record of Bonnie & Carlo's thirty-plus thefts existed?

Yael bit at her lip, chewing on her options. And then it occurred to her that there was at least one theft record she did have access to. She distinctly remembered Falco saying his lieutenant had uncovered the report of an earlier theft that had taken place at the Vatican before 1973. Carlo hadn't been suspected — or he had and then was cleared. But at the very least that meant there had been at least that one other theft to examine.

She wondered why Moreau hadn't mentioned it. Perhaps she

hadn't known. Cornaz very well could have — more likely, *would have.* Given his position, Cornaz was presumably equal to the best of investigators. He might simply have withheld that tidbit from her. Yael couldn't expect Moreau to have known everything Cornaz did. Nor everything he'd done.

The report on that earlier theft was worth looking into if only to understand how they'd ruled out Carlo as the perpetrator. It was possible their conclusions were wrong.

It was more than likely that Falco had maintained this record in his files along with all the other evidence he kept from the investigation of the Magdalene Treasure.

Maybe Yael would find something valuable. After all, Falco and his team hadn't really known the scope of Carlo's crimes, the immense scale of his criminality. They hadn't known about the dozens of counterfeits Bonnie & Carlo had gotten away with up till that point.

CHAPTER 6

*A*fter zig-zagging eight hours from Turin to Rome and then on to Greece, Yael strode into Francesco Falco's house on the isle of Naxos with a sack of groceries slung on her back and roast lamb on her mind.

She hadn't ever cooked for anyone before, except for herself. But Falco wasn't anyone. And so much was new. The whole affair with the Magdalene Treasure had changed her. She felt different. Lighter. Happier. And she simply wanted to do something nice for the dear old man who was losing his mind.

Yael went first to the kitchen and set to work lining everything up on her meal plan. A sumptuous rack of lamb, a host of colorful root vegetables and all the makings of a Horiatiki, the traditional Greek village salad Falco was sure to love.

The matron stood at the chopping block. "The old man has taken to living in his den," she said in her native tongue. "He never moves from that place. Not since you left. Sleeps on the chair. He has grown more distant. Lost on the sea."

The news saddened Yael. "Will he eat?" she asked.

"A little. If he is fed."

"Is he lucid?" Yael asked.

The woman pursed her lips, tears pooling her eyes. "No. But he's more at peace than ever before. It is hard for me, yes. But for him? I think it is good."

By the time Yael crept into the basement room, Falco was dozing quietly on his recliner. Such a sweet man. She'd been looking forward to seeing him. Maybe joining him on another adventure through time.

Yael placed her hand gently on his head. His lids fluttered revealing a slice of his eyes, but it was clear they were vacant. A man adrift on his sea.

Yael sucked in her breath and went to the far end of the lair, to the shelves holding the file boxes she had seen just a few days before. It didn't take long to dig out the report on the solo Vatican theft which had occurred years before the theft of the Magdalene Treasure.

The report was thorough. In 1971 the Vatican Museums had been accused of negligence in their handling of a rare and priceless manuscript composed by the legendary thirteenth-century Sufi mystic and poet Jalal-ad-Din Rumi in honor of his spiritual teacher and friend.

The manuscript, entitled *Divan-e Kabir*, was owned by the Aga Khan, heir to a religious dynasty, royal titles, and storied wealth. He'd also inherited the scandalous reputation of a wanton playboy from his grandfather and his father — men who'd taken to models, actresses, dancers, prancers, and vixens like spoilt brats to a toy store.

According to the original Vatican report, Divan-e Kabir was kept in a vault that had been specifically designed to preserve collectible paintings, documents, and textiles. The vault's security was managed by an agent of the insurance company that insured the contents.

The appraisal of the piece had been ordered by the insurer in 1958 when the vault was first built and was conducted again in 1971 for the purpose of an enhanced policy. The appraiser in 1971 realized quickly that the Sufi manuscript was a counterfeit.

The security agent was able to confirm that the only time the document had been vulnerable to compromise was in the spring of 1968 when the Vatican Museums had been engaged to repair moisture damage from centuries before. Ultimately, it hadn't mattered who was to blame, because the Vatican's insurer was the same as the Aga Khan's. So the loss had been paid.

The Vatican report detailed that Georges Markel, the Gendarmerie Chief at the time—presumably the man who'd held the post before Cornaz was brought in to shake things up in 1973—had studied the Aga Khan's security protocols and found no fault with them. He'd subsequently initiated a thorough investigation of all personnel at the Vatican Museums but never found the culprit.

Yael looked through the notes. There was no record of Carlo ever having been questioned. And yet Falco had told her he'd been cleared.

How could that be? After all, Carlo had joined the Vatican in '65, placing him directly where he needed to be '68 when the Divan-e Kabir was in reach.

CHAPTER 7

*Y*ael turned to her computer tablet to access the copy of Carlo's employee file that Tech had electronically produced when she'd first come across his name. Tech was her trusty dark web genius who could pull rabbits out of hats with the best of them — most often better.

There was little of value in the employment record. Only the barest of details remained. It was just one page and contained nothing close to what might be expected of an employee file. It had likely been redacted in 1973, because, as Moreau had said, Carlo's counterfeiting-thefts were an embarrassment to the Vatican. And so his record had been scrubbed clean, the stain of his transgressions best kept hidden from history and the world.

But Yael was not deterred. She dug through the evidence boxes until she found the files that Falco had collected in '73 of all of the Vatican Museum staff who'd been employed at the time of the theft. She set aside the stack of documents related to the non-Vatican experts and visiting scholars associated with the museum and honed in on the employees until she found Carlo's full and un-redacted employment record.

She'd barely begun reading when the anomaly leapt right off the page. After completing his second year at the Vatican, Carlo had taken a sabbatical to study advanced valuation methods with the New York Metropolitan Museum of Art. A checkmark sat alongside the notation of a conference he'd participated in while at the Met that neatly book-ended the dates the Aga Khan's book had been at the Vatican. Beneath the check, *ATTENDANCE CONFIRMED* was scrawled in red ink along with the initials CV. That would be Carmine Vespucci, Falco's trusted lieutenant.

Carlo had been in New York at the time, which meant he couldn't have stolen it. But that didn't make sense. The Divan-e Kabir was a manuscript, which placed it very much in Bonnie & Carlo's wheel-house of Papers. On top of that—

Unless! In Carlo's absence, *Bonnie* had committed the theft. It made sense. If true, it meant that somehow Bonnie must have been affiliated with the Vatican too.

Yael was inclined to trust Falco's conclusions that the Vatican women they'd questioned in '73 had been properly vetted — suffi-ciently enough to rule out Bonnie's presence back then. Yet Bonnie had to have been at the Vatican when Carlo was in New York in '68. How else had she had the kind of access she'd needed to replicate and steal the Aga Khan's book?

Yael gushed with delight. She could hardly contain her fascination with this woman. It was already strong and now only growing.

Yael was well aware that she had an aversion to all forms of authority, whether that came in the form of men or teachers or Indian warrior gurus — whatever their social academic or religious perver-sions might be. And Bonnie was an example to her of a bold and free spirit, free from the confines of the paradigms of norm. How amazing would it have been to know her?

If only.

CHAPTER 8

*F*alco was resting peacefully in his chair. Matron was watching the stove and doing whatever else it was that she did as long as it was away from the den. Yael had instructed her to steer clear while she put her mind to Carlo's mysterious criminal partner.

But Yael had nothing to go on in her search for Bonnie. This meant that although Carlo was quite literally a dead lead, he was certainly worth pursuing. After all, Yael was now armed with the knowledge of a slew of other thefts that predated the events of '73. The stakes had changed. She was faced with the possibility that those other precious objects were still out there unrecovered — either the actual stolen goods or the riches Bonnie & Carlo had amassed upon selling them.

Yael didn't really want to go over ground that had already been cleared from Falco's investigation, but then how thorough had their search of Carlo been in '73? Things had happened so quickly. And before they'd known it, Carlo was dead and the Treasure destroyed.

Yael quickly found the box containing the files on Carlo Rinaldi and dove in. As she looked through the documents she remembered

Falco saying that before he'd taken over the investigation of the theft of the Treasure, Gendarmerie Chief Cornaz had led the charge.

Carlo was the early suspect, and Cornaz had initiated a frontal attack, assisted by the local Carabinieri. They had searched Carlo's home and interrogated his family and friends. At the time they had a singular focus, to locate their missing curator.

When Falco had come on board, he'd put an immediate stop to the aggressive manhunt. Presumably, because such tactics stood to place the Treasure at risk. Falco had redirected the efforts to amass information on Carlo. Anything about his life and lifestyle. And any known haunts.

Falco's purpose was to know who he was dealing with. Vespucci had assembled a neat file on the man, though they seemed to have done nothing with it once the events of the ransom exchange had begun to unfold.

But Falco hadn't known then what Yael knew now. That in addition to the Magdalene Treasure there were another thirty or so valuable pieces of art at stake that Carlo had also stolen.

Yael studied the files closely. She was impressed at how much Vespucci had been able to dig up without causing the ripples that might have altered Carlo's set-course with the ransom exchange. It was 1973, years before such information would have been accessible in anything other than paper form or through direct questioning of those who knew of him and his affairs. For Yael, it served to underscore Vespucci's prowess and cement his rightful position as Falco's Number One.

As Yael read through the papers, a picture began to form in her mind of who Carlo Rinaldi really was. It appeared he had come from a good family in the interior countryside of Le Marche in eastern Italy. Carlo was the youngest of eight. He had been an athlete, a promising goalkeeper in football — soccer, as it was known in America. He'd been drawn into a junior league at the age of nine, and it was this engagement and the associated travel early in his life that bolstered his confidence and opened doors for him, ultimately earning him a place in a university.

His parents and each of his siblings had remained in the village and lived a simple life which Carlo had modestly supported once he'd become an earner. It was a time when fifty dollars or the equivalent in Italian lira would have gone a long way. Carlo was charming, confident and intelligent. He'd never married and had no children — at least none that they'd found. As for relationships, the list had been long.

Yael took another swipe at Carlo's employee file. The man had been living on what she imagined was a modest salary in '73. The police report from Cornaz' raid had bolstered that, describing Carlo's apartment as a tiny one-bedroom in a run-down building. It was inconsistent with him being a wealthy thief. At least *visibly* so.

Then her eye caught the notation added to his file in 1968 when Carlo was on sabbatical at the New York Met. Yael stared at the swanky Manhattan address they'd recorded. There was no way whether now or fifty years ago that such a home could be afforded on a museum curator's salary. And his family certainly didn't have that kind of money.

Finally, she had some proof of his spoils.

CHAPTER 9

Suddenly, a heavenly flash lit up the darkened room. Yael's heart jumped. A moment later the not-so-distant blast of a thousand bombs rocked the den. Lightning and thunder — somewhere out at sea. The melted Bronze Globe toppled from its perch on the mantle.

Falco's lids flipped open, and the frail old man trembled as if cowering in fear at the rage of the Gods.

The Pancake, as Yael had called the Globe before she knew what it was, now lay on the floor at her feet. In the center was some kind of a stubby, steel tripod that must have served to secure its mass to the wall above the mantle. It was too heavy to lift comfortably in her hands. And yet according to the Gospel of J, Mary Magdalene had once held this Sacred Bronze Globe herself.

Yael sat staring at it for what felt like a really long time. Had it really been delivered by Jesus? Into the hands of Mary Magdalene? How could it possibly have survived two thousand years only to be haphazardly reduced to a molten bauble?

It was this last thought that caused Yael's breathing to quicken. She rose from her knees and went on a hunt through the case files. She dug until she came to the pictures capturing the scene of the explosion that had incinerated both the Treasure and the thieves.

In the back of the van, the Globe could be seen melted to a puddle. The steel tripod was visible in the center of the bronze. How odd. Yael looked over to the same ugly pancake lying on the floor in front of her.

The fire in the van had burned hot enough and long enough to completely melt the bronze right to its core, leaving the tripod embedded within. But where had that steel bracket come from?

And what about the bodies in the front of the van?

Yael flipped through more of the crime scene pictures. The camera had captured the only clear closeup photo of Bonnie. It would make most anyone wretch. But not Yael.

Strangely, the grisly corpse had been pictured still upright in its seat, as was Carlo's body. The explosion must have been instantaneous. Bonnie & Carlo hadn't even had time to move, let alone escape. They were burned beyond recognition. Only heavily charred flesh remained.

Yael stopped dead in her tracks. How could that be? She plugged some figures into her phone and searched. Given the expected intensity of the explosion and the heat of the fire, it was surprising the bodies hadn't been completely stripped to the bone.

Yet they hadn't. Which meant there was no way that the Globe could have melted so fully — not without consuming the flesh. In addition, for the bronze to have pooled as it had, the bodies should have been well on the way to skeletal cremation.

It just didn't fit.

Yael racked her brain trying to think of any possible cause for the anomaly. She pressed her fingertips to her temples. Try as she might, she could find only one viable conclusion.

The bronze was already melted before the van had exploded.

There had to have been an accident *before* the accident.

CHAPTER 10

*a*n accident before the accident. And yet that made no sense at all. Because if so, Bonnie & Carlo would have strayed far from the final exchange.

It left only one possibility. The melting hadn't been an accident. Bonnie & Carlo had destroyed the Sacred Bronze Globe intentionally.

Yael pondered this. What had their agenda been? They'd swapped the olive box concealing base concrete instead of the Bronze Globe for the ten million dollars in the blue basket. It was a game-changer, a brilliant ruse that they'd gotten away with.

But then why had they melted the Globe before pretending to exchange it?

Unless it wasn't the Globe but simply made to appear so.

Yael examined the bronze pancake more closely. It was peppered with small *rock-candy* jewels. How could she know for certain it was fake? The bronze metal itself would have been easy enough to fabricate, especially since no casting was required. It was nothing more than a melted glob. But the embedded gems, although quite small, looked very real. Old and uncut, like ancient jewels often were.

And then it struck her. Yael reached for the missing and stolen items report again. She rifled quickly through the pages until she came to the year 1975. There it was, the listing for the scepter Moreau had told Yael about.

She read down to the description recorded of the gems on the scepter's haft and compared it to what she saw on the pancake. They matched perfectly, all but two gems described in the theft report that were missing on the Pancake — an emerald and a black sapphire. Perhaps they'd be found embedded beneath the surface.

Regardless, the meaning was clear. The Pancake was not the real Bronze Globe. The rock-candy had been lifted right off the stolen scepter.

Yael laughed aloud at her discovery. No one had thought to question the evidence. To confirm if the Pancake was really the Globe. But back then they didn't have the means to verify it really, other than the sketch that accompanied the ransom letter and whatever description the first Cardinal Sideris would have given Falco.

Carlo Rinaldi had been the only one with full knowledge of the Bronze, and he was the thief. On top of that, the investigation had been cut short the day following the failed final exchange, and Falco had been ordered to dispose of any and all evidence. Any due diligence he might normally have exercised to rule out a ruse had been halted.

The thieves hadn't bothered to replicate the Globe. It wasn't their specialty. Not sculptures. Not castings. And certainly not bronze.

Which explained the theft of the scepter—also not a Paper—without a replica being left in its place. It had been stolen strictly for the purpose of serving to counterfeit the Globe. And since Carlo was clearly the scepter's thief, it served to unambiguously reaffirm his role in the theft of the Magdalene Treasure.

Yael's eyes were drawn to Falco's precious Ducati-Sogno camera and the metal box it had rested atop on the mantle. Both had also fallen to the floor when the thunder felled the Pancake. Ashes spilled out from the open lid of the lead case.

Yael's mind was connecting dots quickly now. The bronze on the pancake which had been the bronze in the van wasn't the bronze from the Globe. Ergo, it would be fair to presume that the ashes from the lead box found in the van which she was surely looking at right now weren't the cinders from the Codex. In other words, this lead box was not an urn.

The Treasure had survived! Both items, the Bronze Globe as well as the Magdalene Prophecy.

Yael turned to see Francesco sound asleep in his chair. It was a good thing he was gone. She wasn't sure she wanted to share this discovery with him. It might break the little left unbroken in his heart.

And while the Treasure had survived the classified events of '73, the real tragedy had been what happened to the thieves. Bonnie & Carlo had died senselessly in an unfortunate accident. Their brilliantly crafted criminal charade had ended in flames. What incredible boldness they must have had to expect to get away with such a ruse.

Yael sucked in a huge breath as the import of her discovery sunk in.

Today's ransom letter was real.

Whoever sent it was somehow connected to Bonnie & Carlo.

The Treasure was still out there.

And someone wanted a deal.

CHAPTER 11

*Y*ael thought of the masterminds. Bonnie & Carlo had been highly-successful, prolific thieves well before the events of '73 — so good, in fact, that their thefts had escaped notice for years and years.

Then came the Magdalene Treasure. With a value of a hundred million dollars, it would have been the grab of a lifetime. But it was obvious that Bonnie & Carlo's last caper had strayed from their past successes. It wasn't a theft hidden by counterfeits. The MO was new — a theft for ransom.

And yet it was abundantly clear that they had never intended to *exchange* the Treasure. The bronze Pancake staged in the back of the van proved that.

Yael let the ramifications of this sink in. First, the thieves had traded a concrete-laden wooden box in lieu of the Globe in exchange for a ten-million-dollar gift basket. Why hadn't they simply disappeared after that? They had the Magdalene Treasure intact and a hefty sum in their jeans. What else did they have to gain by going to the final exchange?

The answer was obvious — the remaining ninety million dollars, of course. But had it really been worth such a risk? Hindsight said no.

So what had they planned? One final deception, that much was sure. The Pancake staged in the back of the van was proof enough they had more up their sleeve.

Had they planned to trigger an explosion after trading the van and its contents? If so, it had been brilliant and oafish at the same time. Brilliant for obvious reasons. Oafish because they'd been caught in their own convolution, killed in what most likely was nothing more than a reckless and premature explosion.

Bonnie & Carlo were dead. At least that much was true.

Yael now had to wonder what in truth the duo had intended next if their van *hadn't* caught fire. Until their deaths, their plan had been flawless. And clever.

They'd needed the time to make it work. The time to plan the events that unfolded. The time to set things up. The time to create the counterfeit Codex. It explained why a seemingly-simple ransom exchange had taken weeks to come together. They'd counted on the delays to buy them the time.

But then calamity struck. They died just seconds from the bridge where Falco was waiting. The route they'd been on when the van had exploded confirmed they were in fact on their way to face off on the bridge. Falco had made this explicitly clear.

And now Yael was certain that the Pancake was already melted by the time of the meet. So had they crafted a counterfeit of the Codex as well?

The question still lingered. How had Bonnie & Carlo intended to make it appear as if they were trading the real Bronze Globe along with the Codex for the final sum?

The bulk of the bronze pancake must have been pre-melted in order to account for what he'd expect to find — the remnants of a solid bronze sphere.

Yael pondered the puzzle, playing into the scheming minds of the pair. It was possible Bonnie & Carlo had crafted a *hollow* bronze globe with the specter's gems that would have passed from a distance. It could easily have been staged atop a flammable platform—perhaps a sheet—that hid the melted bronze from sight. A thin bronze veneer painted over a balloon would have melted easily enough.

CHAPTER 12

The puzzle pieces were starting to fit. Now Yael imagined how the final exchange might have gone down.

She pictured Bonnie & Carlo parked on one end of the bridge so they could easily escape if things went wrong. Bonnie stayed in the van in order to conceal her identity.

Yael imagined Carlo walking midway onto the bridge to where Falco was waiting to confront him with his discovery that the Wooden Box was lacking its bronze pearl. Carlo defended his actions to Falco, arguing a little eye-for-an-eye, retribution for Falco having played them when he had short-changed their initial demand.

Yael could picture Carlo walk Falco back to the van to view the fake Globe, which had been carefully secured to the floor with the steel anchor bolt the picture had revealed. Carlo then presented the Codex briefly before returning it to Bonnie, with whom it would remain until he verified receipt of the balance of the ransom.

The two men then walked to the payphone at the far end of the bridge, the one Falco mentioned when he first told his story. Falco and Carlo each took turns calling their banks, Falco to give final transfer instructions for the ninety million dollars and Carlo to confirm receipt.

Once back in the midpoint of the bridge, they exchanged car keys and separated. Falco went to the van and the supposed Treasure, while Bonnie joined Carlo in Falco's car.

Yael assumed it was then that Bonnie & Carlo would have triggered the explosion in order to destroy the fake Treasure. Whether they'd intended to do that before or after Falco reached the van would have spoken a lot to whether their criminality transcended mere thievery.

But this is where things stopped adding up for Yael. Bonnie & Carlo's getaway was flawed.

They couldn't possibly have anticipated what remedies Falco had planned. As soon as Falco was in possession of the Treasure or what he believed was the Treasure, he could easily call for the bridge to be stormed from either end by officers who by then would have had ample time to get into place. It didn't wash. Something was missing.

What Yael did know was that while the Magdalene Treasure had survived the explosion, Bonnie & Carlo had not. And now decades later, someone had sent the next in the series of ransom letters drafted in '73. Whoever this person was had to be connected somehow to Bonnie & Carlo. And they had to know where the Treasure was. The challenge was in finding them.

There was no real evidence to speak of. No autopsy examinations had ever been done. Dental records, surgical history, and any other such avenues would remain forever unexplored, as would a slew of highly effective modern tests that had not existed back in the day.

That ship had quite literally sailed with Falco at the helm into the Tyrrhenian Sea, the frenzied feeding ground of the old man's trusty sharks.

CHAPTER 13

*I*t was the very end of another dark, happening night. Matron had served them dinner in the den and stayed to feed Falco. Then she'd retired to clean up in the kitchen.

Falco was once again sitting idly staring into the fire. Yael wasn't so sure who she was seeing, his mother's child, a brilliant inspector out of his time or simply a befuddled, old man.

There was little more Yael could learn here. She had a new mission, to hunt the sender of today's ransom demand — her new mark. The envelope bore the number 17 of 24, making it the very next number in the series of 16 that had been received at the Vatican in '73.

So whoever sent it had Bonnie & Carlo's things. The bottom line — it had to be someone connected to them long ago. And since finding out anything about Bonnie was a non-starter, once again Yael was back to Carlo. With no other leads, digging into his past was the right place to start in search of her mark.

Yael had already booked herself on the early-morning flight to Rome. In twenty minutes she'd leave for the airport. As she was tidying up, returning each of the files to their respective boxes and the boxes to their set place on the far wall, she paused to take in the grue-some picture of Bonnie's corpse one final time.

The sight of it struck a chord with Yael. The melted flesh had rendered it completely unrecognizable. And at that moment it occurred to her that there was still one other place where Bonnie's image would have been captured.

Yael reached over to the remote control on Falco's chair-side table and powered on the VCR and TV. She dug out the old surveillance video cassette from Falco's investigation and popped it in. The televi-sion screen flashed to a bright blue screen.

She sat back and hit PLAY. The VCR churned. The screen showed snow. And suddenly the churning grew louder. Something was wrong. Yael hit STOP quickly, leaned forward and pressed the EJECT button on the front of the machine. The cassette was dutifully released along with a tangled mess of dark tinted film-tape.

"Damn thing's broken," she muttered in anger.

"Don't worry," the Matron murmured in Greek from the doorway.

How long had she been there?

"My son will fix it," she said, coming into the room. "The old man used to watch it all the time. He wore out the machine and the tape."

"I'd like to take it with me," Yael said, holding the unspooled cassette.

"Here," Matron said, reaching for an SD card plugged into the TV. "It is all there. My son did it for Francesco. You can take this. My son will make another copy from his computer."

Before leaving, Yael wrote a brief note to Falco promising to return as soon as she could, knowing he would probably never read it. Then she rushed off to catch her plane.

$\sim$

*A*t the tiny airport's security station, Marco's satchel was dumped out on a stainless steel table.

"My flight boards soon," Yael said to the man pawing through her things. "What are you looking for?"

The greasy agent glanced up at Yael but didn't answer.

"I'm a diplomat," she said, showing the fake UN badge with the alias she'd been using for the past few weeks. "And I'm in a rush."

The man lazily studied Alexis Keaton's ID, before shrugging and stuffing the items back into the bag.

"Don't!" she said sharply, yanking the satchel from his hands and slinging it across her shoulder. Two items remained on the table. She tucked the Vat's library book containing the painting from the ransom letter's stamp into the satchel and spun away, leaving the trash on the table.

"Take it with you," the security agent said, pointing to a courier envelope she'd discarded.

"There's nothing in it!" she glared, slapping her hand hard down for effect, as she picked it up and strode away.

Idiot!

CHAPTER 14

*A*t the gate, Yael stood back and watched while the passengers lined up for the flight. No sense in rushing only to have everyone behind her jostle and bump and then stare as they passed by her seat at the front of the plane.

She'd much rather be the one watching from behind as they all shuffled on board. It was one of those rare situations where Yael felt a person's true nature emerged. And so she'd look to see who was aggressive, who was impatient, who was gracious and who was indifferent as each one lined up to be inspected, approved and sent down the gangplank.

Among the very first in line was a tall, slender woman around the same age as Yael who oozed an aura of wealth and privilege. She wore a broad-brimmed black hat, dark round sunglasses, and bright red lipstick. There was a circle painted on her chin. *How Cindy Crawford!* Her black dress was cut short above the knee and clung tightly to her olive-tanned form.

Yael's own sundress flowed softly without hiding her curves. But it didn't hold a candle to the skintight wrap she'd snared in her sights.

The woman wasn't quite pornographic. Nor was she quite *un*-pornographic. But she was undeniably, incredibly sexy.

Yael wasn't the only one looking. Most of the men had been struck by Pavlov's bell. The women stared too, although they managed to hide it better. Yael watched in delight when a ruffled young mother trying to board early with a toddler in her arms had to turn back for her six-year-old boy who'd abandoned his tiny suitcase and was standing entranced in front of the bare-legged enchantress.

A short while later when all were aboard, Yael strolled into First Class.

"Merde!" the stunning woman in black yelled out. Her champagne went flying and splashed the man in the seat behind her.

"There is a bumblebee flying about!" she yelled in an angry yet funnily-sweet French accent. "These ridiculous old planes!"

The woman was still behind dark specs but had traded her hat for a delicate silk scarf. *Damn the paparazzi!* Where did she think they were? Hollywood?

Yael stood in the aisle, while the flight attendant crouched by the woman.

"I'm very sorry, ma'am. Are you okay? Were you stung?"

"No, not *stung!*" she said emphatically. "But I do not *want* to be stung!"

The pilot appeared and apologized to the woman while the attendant wiped up the champagne and refilled her glass. Then he addressed the passengers in the curtained-off fore-cabin.

"Does anybody see the bumblebee?"

"There's no bee," snapped the man with champagne on his face as he mopped his bald pate with the hot towel he'd been given.

"Very sorry sir," the pilot said kindly. "If anyone does see anything flying about, please alert my crew immediately. I'm sorry for the disturbance."

Yael stood chuckling within. This was turning into such a fun trip!

CHAPTER 15

*Y*ael had taken her seat at the window with the French tart at her right and quickly donned blinders. Once the plane took flight, she caught sight of the empty courier envelope dangling from where she'd tucked it earlier in the seat-back pocket stuffed with magazines and vomit sacks.

She slid the waybill from the plastic window. It was addressed to Cardinal Sideris and bore a bright red *RECEIVED* stamp dated the same day Yael had been called to the Vatican to investigate the receipt of the ransom demand.

It was then that she noticed what was written in the *Description* section of the waybill, *17 of 24.* It was the very same curious notation that had been penned on the ransom envelope.

Suddenly, it dawned on Yael as if—like the plane had just done—she'd risen through the obscurity of clouds to a bright new horizon. She had just discovered how the ransom letter had been sent to Sideris!

The Sender's name was obscure. *DLO.* No address. Just Atlanta, Georgia.

Yael slid her eye mask back down and watched the clouds. The global hub for Delta Airlines was in Atlanta. DLO was possibly an acronym for one of their divisions. Delta Operations, no doubt.

The trajectory of what had begun as a curiosity trip was now dramatically changed. First, she'd learned that the Treasure had survived the explosion in '73, despite the fact that Bonnie & Carlo had not.

And now Yael had a lead to the intrepid thieves' surviving heir. The inheritor of their fortune. The person who'd sent the ransom letter. The person who surely still had the Magdalene Treasure.

~

She might have dozed because the next thing she felt was someone hovering. Yael lifted her blindfold.

The flight attendant smiled. "We'll be serving breakfast shortly. Have you decided whether you'd like the omelette or the continental?"

"No," said Yael, sliding the mask back into place.

Barely seconds had passed before a sharp slap on her leg and an even sharper sting jerked Yael from her reverie. She recoiled in pain, throwing off her eye shield. But a foreign hand was gripping firmly to her thigh. It was connected to the French woman beside her who now was yelling.

"The Bumblebee! *Mon Dieu!* Again the bumblebee!"

The flight attendant came running as Yael forced the woman's hand from her leg. There on her inside-right thigh just below the hemline was a large red welt with a small bloody puncture. It stung fiercely.

Yael couldn't remember when she'd last been stung by a bee, but it had to be when she was just a girl. She certainly didn't remember it hurting this much.

Yael waved off the flight attendant with the first aid kit. "I'm fine."

Her immune system was strong and would take care of this easily. It was just a bee sting after all.

But while she'd been addressing the attendant, the woman at her side dabbed some ointment on the mark. Yael jerked in response, but the woman persisted, very gently rubbing it in.

"Tiger balm," she said in her now-sweet French voice. "It will calm the sting and reduce the swelling. Permit me."

Her touch was feathery light. And she was right — the pain started to fade. Soon both the redness and swelling were visibly eased.

"Come. Lift your legs. Both of them. Onto my lap," she instructed.

Yael leaned against the window and followed the woman's command. There was no sense arguing. She wouldn't hear of it anyway. And besides, there was something oddly fun about this all.

The woman turned in her seat and pulled Yael's calves onto her so she could easily rub the stung spot. They propped pillows and blankets under Yael's back until she was comfortable.

While all this was happening, Yael noticed the woman's face. She was actually quite beautiful. Strikingly so. In some ways, she looked like a darker-skinned, more elegant version of herself.

"Now, close your eyes. I will take care of you."

Yael did as bade and relaxed while the woman took her in soft, capable hands. Slowly the balm took root, and all pain disappeared.

The woman's fingers drew ticklish circles on her thigh.

"Let us help the blood flow," the woman whispered silkily as her other hand moved high on Yael's thigh and massaged deeply up and down. Side to side. Round and round.

Yael could not quell her arousal and peeked to see the woman behind the shades eyeing her back, a succulent yet saucy pout on her lush red lips. Through the spicy scent of the balm was a waft of vanilla.

Ah, the French, thought Yael as she lay in First Class, legs splayed miles high above the Mediterranean. *Fun, fun, fun!*

~

"M a'am?" said a voice nearby. A hand softly touched Yael's shoulder. "Miss Keaton?"

Yael opened her eyes. Her feet were back on the floor. Miss Magic

Fingers had managed to fall asleep while still sitting erect. The flight attendant was hovering again.

"I'm sorry to disturb you, Miss Keaton. But your seatbelt must be buckled and your seat-back upright. We'll be starting our descent into Rome shortly."

But Yael was in no rush. First Class afforded her that privilege. Instead, she stayed fully reclined, kept her eye mask on and thought of nothing.

~

"*M*iss Keaton?" The attendant was calling again.

Yael looked up, this time portraying the haughty perturbation of the self-important Alexis Keaton, not caring a bit that her earlier French escapade had been so far off-script.

"Would you please return your seat to its upright position and buckle your belt? We are landing now."

Miss Keaton popped out of her seat—deaf to all protestations—and crossed to the lavatory.

Privilege.

CHAPTER 16

*D*arkness had come to Rome as Nellie Coleman walked home from a long day at the museum. It was an unusually warm night and the rose-ringed parakeets were alive in their song.

She crossed a pedestrian bridge that spanned over some railway tracks. She could hear a jogger coming up behind her and moved against the iron railing to her right to make room on the narrow walk.

Nellie had a healthy respect for the level of discipline it took to stay fit, not that she had the same degree of dedication herself. She'd tried it once when she'd first finished school. But by then her cravings for pizza and donuts had taken hold. She was smart enough to figure that with that one domino felled, exercise and moderation stood no chance.

As the runner drew close, Nellie felt a light push on her left shoulder. *Fucker!* She turned to spy the lean physique of a woman dressed in black.

But before she could cast a mean glare, the runner leaped at her with tremendous force, gripping Nellie's shoulders firmly and propelling them both over the guardrail. Together they fell the twenty-plus feet to the coarse gravel below.

Nellie landed with a solid crack flat on her back. Her spine was now in pieces. She felt none of the pain from the breaks in her bones or the stones in her flesh. The call of the parakeets had suddenly grown distant.

The runner had vaulted off Nellie's body mere seconds before impact. She'd somersaulted head over heels, landing on her hands and her feet. As agile as an alley cat. She was now crouched low above Nellie's broken body.

Three shallow breaths passed as Nellie made out the familiar upside-down face she'd spoken to at the Vatican a couple of weeks before.

The very last image Nellie Coleman would capture was of the eyes of the woman staring curiously into her own as what remained of Nellie drained from her life.

∼

*Z*unther Abbot was on the ninth lap of his nightly freestyle ritual. He'd come down to his pool for a swim as his wife went up to their room for an inventory of her bedside drugstore. Zunther would swim long enough for his wife to fade into the pharmaceutical fruit salad she snacked on each night.

She wasn't to blame for his lot. This was his own creation. He'd never loved the woman. She'd only ever had little to offer but her high brow upbringings. That had been more than enough. He'd married purely for the influence her family name would lend. And it had done so in spades, catapulting him to recognition where recognition mattered most and the ultimate prestige of his present position as Director of Vatican Museums.

If not for his work and his most-attentive young assistant, his life would be worth less than the spent shell of the dud bullet he'd once aimed at his head. The woman in his bedroom was a foolish, unthinking, unfeeling, inanimate donkey. He'd repeated it often enough that it now rolled off his mental tongue like ice cream off a child's chin.

And so each night he swam to wash the wretched stink left by his lifeless wife and their fetid life. For Zunther, it was either swim or go in search of a better bullet.

Midway through Zunther's twelfth lap, he thought he heard a splash. A second later, a shadow appeared beneath him in the water. A sharp hand like the pointed fin of a shark thrust out and punched him hard in the gut. Air gushed from his mouth. Before he could turn to draw in more, a pair of legs wrapped tightly around his waist trapping his arms, while hands cinched around his neck. They hugged him close, pulling him down.

He could feel the nakedness of a woman's body as he grappled with death. His chest heaved painfully once, then twice. But he could restrain his lungs no more.

And in that final moment, before Zunther Abbot gasped his last liquid breath, a woman's eyes appeared from the watery shadows and peered into his.

~

*S*ilence to all who know.

~

*E*arlier that same day, an old man had been sitting on a park bench watching the squirrels hanging from branches, scurrying down trunks and scampering for the nuts he'd splayed at his feet. As he bent to set his empty coffee cup down on the ground, he was struck by a burning sensation in his stomach.

To hell with the bitterness he'd just swilled! What had he been reduced to? What self-respecting European in his right mind would drink watered-down coffee through a plastic lid? And what else had he seen? Whipped cream and a straw for the bambini?

The *Americani* made a fortune over-roasting inferior beans and calling them dark. His own paper-cupful had tasted revoltingly bitter and weak and milky and sweet all at once. Despite his disgust, he'd finished the small cup out of respect.

He belched loudly to free the gas from his gut. More than a few heads turned and saw the old man's lips curled in distaste. It hadn't taken long for him to sorely regret having finished the slop.

Less than a minute later, the old man had nothing left of the world to regret. His body spasmed and retched before coming to rest cruelly on the brick paving at the foot of his bench.

It would be a few hours before the coroner identified the old man. The coroner, an Italian first and an espresso aficionado next, took much pleasure in reporting that the final beverage of the aged Greek was a short triple-triple decaf Americano from Starbucks. He'd been able to decrypt this from the paper cup brought in with the body. For the benefit of the report, if not for his own further amusement, the drink was described as *a glorified instantly-brewed decaffeinated coffee with three large dollops each of heavy milk and sugar.*

It would be another few hours before the coroner was able to say with certainty that the man's sudden death was caused by a spoonful of highly-concentrated liquid heroin mixed into his coffee-like bilge.

Witnesses reported that the old man was alone when his seizure had struck but that earlier a young woman had been chatting with him on the bench. She had left before his spasms began, before the old man foamed at the mouth, retched, gagged, convulsed and collapsed.

Sideris the Loyal was dead.

CHAPTER 17

*Y*ael had done what she could with the last of the three bullets Ben had tasked her with — KILL EVERYONE. In continental Europe at least.

Not the old man, though. Not Falco. She was in no mood to stamp out a disheartened young boy that knew her as Mama, no matter his real age. And besides, his dementia had already done the job.

She wouldn't touch the Matron either. Nor her son. Not as long as Falco needed care.

As for London, she was heading there now. She'd left behind a sticky mess made up of Sugar and a few other ingredients. The young student who'd attended to her at Oxford and the Cambridge police would get a pass — even the superintendent. They hadn't learned enough to warrant the risk of taking any one of them out.

Unfortunately, Yael's driver-for-hire was on her hit list. As was Mirabelle *Sugar* Marsi, who Yael was already feeling sorry to have to silence. The woman was likable, despite the trouble she'd caused for Yael, likable possibly even because of it.

Yael would use the three hours in flight to sort out her plan. Once she silenced the three, she'd be free to focus on the personal hunt for her new mark — whoever had breathed new life into the ransom of the Magdalene Treasure.

At the departures level, Yael stepped onto the red carpet reserved for First Class passengers. She was next in line to be checked in for her flight to London. It had been a full day, and she was looking forward to getting off her feet.

As she waited for the First Class counter to clear, she crouched down to examine the bee sting on her leg. It was still sore to the touch, red and inflamed and taking far too long to heal. It made her wonder what kind of bee it had been. Or if it had been a bee at all. Perhaps a wasp or even worse a hornet.

In the economy section, a young American couple was arguing loudly with the airline clerk. Two large knapsacks lay at their feet stuffed to capacity. Rolled up yoga mats and dirty sneakers dangled from the loops on the outside.

Yael was dabbing a liniment of calendula when a voice called out from behind the counter where the young couple was standing. The uniformed agent spoke first in Italian then in English.

"If anyone else is in line for the midnight flight departing to Atlanta, we are sorry to say that check-in closed twenty minutes ago."

Atlanta? Could it be?

Yael walked up to the male ticketing agent whose counter had cleared. He was a rotund man with a big pudge of face and large, roving eyes. She bent low as if to fiddle with her bag, letting her blouse sag through the neckline and reveal her bare chest. She angled her face up and smiled at the round man who was now wearing a toothsome, schoolboy grin. Her arrows had hit their mark.

"Get me on that flight to Atlanta," she purred. "First Class."

CHAPTER 18

*S*omewhere across the Atlantic, Yael dug out the SD Card that Falco's Matron had given her. If only the surveillance video would show something—*anything*—to reveal who Bonnie was. The chances were slim. Falco's investigators had studied it thoroughly years before. And she knew that Vespucci's keen eye couldn't possibly have overlooked something that significant.

But Yael was undeterred. At the very least, she'd catch a glimpse of the thieving pair in action. She could see how they interacted with each other. Maybe she'd spot something in their stance, in their pace, in their confidence or lack of it. Who knew what it might reveal? At the very least it would give her a feel for who they had been.

The screen on Yael's device showed a long list of files in the SD Card's folder. It took just a few clicks to realize that what she had was much more than she thought. The Matron's son had apparently digitized *all* of Falco's investigation files. Not just the videos.

One caught her eye, a document marked *RE CARDINAL SIDERIS — FOR YOUR EYES ONLY*. It had been prepared by Vespucci for Falco alone and reported on Sideris's activities leading up to his discovery of the theft of the Magdalene Treasure.

There was nothing new that Falco hadn't already told Yael when she'd first learned of the theft, with one exception. According to Vespucci, in 1973 Adolfos Sideris had maintained two offices. The first was in the general chambers housing the apartments and offices of many of the bishops in residence at the Vatican. His second office was the one that caught Yael off guard.

It was at the Vatican Bank, the same place where Cardinal Panos Sideris occupied an office today. *Strange odds,* Yael mused. The two men seemed to share more than just the same name.

It brought to mind another question that hadn't fully formed in her mind until now. What was Ben's connection to the Vatican? Of all possible investigators, why had Ben been drawn into an investigation that in all rights fell under the jurisdiction of the Vatican Gendarmerie?

A very similar thing had happened in 1973. The Gendarmerie had been pulled from the case by someone in a position of authority at the Vatican. In their place, Francesco Falco had been installed. Falco was at the time a Special Investigator of the GdF, an elite division of the Italian Military Police dealing with financial crimes, smuggling, and illegal narcotics.

These were clear and incontrovertible patterns Yael hadn't pieced together so clearly before this moment. Adolfos Sideris had been the person of influence at the Vatican in '73 who'd sidestepped the Gendarmerie in favor of Falco. And in the same vein, it made sense that Panos Sideris himself had made the decision to seek out Ben Saba when he'd received the ransom demand rather than report directly to the Vatican police.

Another fact came to mind. In Ben's initial assignment briefs to Yael, he'd clearly stated that the Vatican was not their client — and no one at the Vatican other than Sideris was to be engaged in the investigation.

And of course, the question still remained, of all the possible choices at his avail, why had Sideris contacted Ben Saba to handle the ransom demand? Sideris *the Loyal,* as Ben had tagged him.

Yael stretched her arms and legs in opposite directions and power-fully arched her back. This was all very interesting, but there was something more pressing. She scrolled through the SD card's folder and opened the lone video file.

The screen quickly filled with moving images made from ancient lenses and static cameras captured on poor film. It hadn't been edited beyond the relevant bits having been strung together by Falco's team.

Yael watched the rough images without the benefit of sound, music, or subtitles. And yet somehow she was completely enrapt as the incredible theft of the Magdalene Treasure unfolded before her eyes.

The early part of the video showed visitors coming into the Vatican the morning of the theft. That would have been on Monday, November 26, 1973. The only thing unusual Yael spotted was a boy dashing through St. Peter's Square like he was catching a train.

She also saw a young mother pushing a stroller. A little girl walked beside her, one hand on the stroller, the other secure in her father's grip. The stroller had three balloons strung to it. It reminded Yael of the balloons which had been used by Bonnie & Carlo in their caper — first over the Vatican Gardens carrying their message of a revised ransom deal and second floating above the wooden box supposedly containing the Bronze Globe on the first phase of the final exchange.

She leaned into the screen when she first caught sight of the wheelchair that carried a pregnant Bonnie. Carlo was at the helm. Their faces weren't visible, and Yael found herself trying to make out details that just weren't there. If there were only some way the images could be enhanced.

Bonnie was shielded behind sunglasses and a scarf. Carlo was wearing a ball cap. His stride seemed to convey both strength and confidence, not the wild panic that might be expected of a young man carrying his pregnant wife to the hospital.

Yael followed Bonnie being wheeled against the stream of visitors at a very fast clip, turning the heads of those around them. As they neared the exit, Carlo bounced the wheelchair down a couple of steps.

Yael laughed. Witnesses to the event were visibly horrified to see a pregnant woman in labor suffer such abuse.

There was no doubt in Yael's mind — she was definitely watching Bonnie & Carlo executing the theft of a lifetime.

CHAPTER 19

*T*hanks to the courtesy given to diplomats, Yael breezed
through Customs and Immigration at Atlanta's Hartsfield-
Jackson International. The less privileged were suffering the noto-
rious craziness of America's busiest airport.

She didn't have to go too far to find the offices of Delta
Operations.

"I need to track a shipment," she said to the woman at the counter.

"This isn't shipping and cargo, ma'am. But let's see if I can help
you." Her fingers clicked rhythmically on the terminal. She seemed to
be moving through a number of screens.

Finally, she looked up. "Do you have the tracking number?"

Yael read it out slowly.

"Hmm," the woman said, scrunching her mouth. "That's not working. Was this commercial or private? And a box or a pallet?"

"Just an envelope."

"Oh, well that explains it. Everything under 150 pounds is shipped
through UPS. I can track it in their system." She punched more keys.
"The tracking number again, please?"

As the woman plugged it in, her face scrunched again. "Are you
sure you have the right number?"

Yael slid the waybill across the counter.

"Oh! This explains it!" the woman said. "This is a waybill for the *USPS*, not UPS."

"But it was sent by you," Yael said.

"A lot of people get confused. We ship with UPS, the United Parcel Service. This was sent by the USPS, the United States Postal Service."

"Yes, but I mean the Sender was you. Delta Operations."

"Oh," said the woman, examining the waybill again. "Well, that's the problem right there. This wasn't sent by Delta. DLO stands for the Dead Letter Office. It's a division of the US Post where all the mail goes that can't be delivered."

⌇

*T*wo-and-a-half hours later, Yael was standing at the DLO service counter inside a windowless, lifeless, grey room. She'd been waiting in line for 40 minutes. The rest of the time had been lost to the insanity of Atlanta traffic.

The postal officer in front of her could have been in a cartoon. His belly overhung a too-tightly-cinched belt on what looked like a pair of adolescent slim-fit slacks. He'd searched the shipment on his computer and now looked at Yael through fancy green-framed glasses.

"The addressee is a Cardinal at the Vatican," he said, sounding bored.

"I can see that," said Yael. "It's on the waybill."

"Yes, that's correct," he said, not making sense.

"Okay. And who was the sender?"

"The Dead Letter Office."

"No, I mean, who was the original sender?"

"That's not on this screen," he said.

"Is there another screen?"

"Yes. I can't access that."

"Who can?"

"I can. But not without a warrant."

"This is an urgent matter for the Vatican."

"So?" he said.

Yael pulled out her Interpol badge and flashed it for effect.

"I understand," he said. "You're important."

Still, he remained staring blankly at Yael.

"Can't you just help?"

"I won't. Not without a warrant."

Yael's frustration was building, but the postal clerk seemed to be quite unruffled by the exchange. He was textbook—almost robotic—in his responses and seemed to be in no hurry to get on to anything else. He probably could have continued this empty dialogue with her until his shift ended or at least until the lunch bell rang.

"Can I speak to the supervisor."

"That's me," he said without blinking.

"Do *you* have a supervisor I can speak to?"

"She'll tell you the same thing."

"Can I please speak to her?"

"She's busy."

"And I'm Interpol."

He tapped some keys on his computer. Yael watched through the reflection on the man's glasses as the screen went blank. Then he disappeared around a corner. Yael leaned over the counter to be sure and saw the login prompt flashing. *Damn!*

A minute later the man reappeared. He walked slowly all the way toward Yael until his belly touched the counter. Only then did he speak.

"The shift supervisor is just going on her break."

"Really. She won't see me now," Yael said blandly. She wasn't asking, just restating the obvious for effect.

"Things move slowly here," he said.

Slowly? No fuck! The thought caused her to wonder how slowly.

"Okay," she said, lifting her hands in surrender. "Can you tell me how long this would have been with you before it was forwarded to the Vatican?"

"I can't access that," he said.

"Well, generally," she said. "How long does it take to process the stuff that comes in here?"

"Weeks. Maybe months. There's a mountain back there," he said. "You'll need to come back in 30 minutes."

Yael looked over her shoulder at the long line of people waiting behind her. She felt sorry for them.

"Can I just wait here on the side?" she said nodding to the wall full of posters.

"If you like."

"Will she call me when she's back from her break?"

"No. You'll need to get in line again."

Yael couldn't tell whether she was seeing smugness on his face or just complete indifference, but she was so angry she might easily have resembled a cartoon character with steam pouring from her ears.

The man was ridiculous, but she knew it would be useless—likely defeating— to challenge him. The only thing she was left wondering was if he was even aware of how difficult he was being.

Was he simply responding to the way he'd been trained? Or was he just another of the really stupid people America was so good at breeding?

CHAPTER 20

A short while later Yael had slipped into her workout clothes and was running through the paved pathways of Piedmont Park. The lush green of the grassy fields soothed her as the sun bounced off downtown Atlanta's towering backdrop.

Her visit to the Dead Letter Office had been a bust. A stupid waste of time, when time was very much of the essence. After all, the stakes were high.

The 1973 ransom demand for the Magdalene Treasure had been initiated anew after an almost-fifty year gap. Yael knew that if she found the sender, one way or another she'd be sure to find the Treasure.

Although Ben had waved her off the matter after she'd learned the supposed fate of the Treasure from Falco, Yael had persisted, fueled simply by curiosity. And said persistence had paid off in spades.

Yael was now pursuing the Magdalene Treasure. Not for Ben. For herself. Not for the many hundreds of millions of dollars it might fetch. For the possibility of the incredible *more* that was at stake.

She'd never before dreamt of crossing Ben or doing anything to counter his directives. But she was no longer fixated on Ben above all or on her blind obeisance to his authority.

Yael felt different. For starters, she'd begun to see that her life was hers, and she was free to choose her course. Thomas had made the difference. It was in observing the effortless ease with which he lived his life that Yael had seen that same possibility for herself.

She had uncovered an intimacy within her that she hadn't known before. It was as if Thomas had opened her to a tenderness she'd long kept hidden, as if he was chiseling the hard shell she'd formed out of the tragic ash of her early life.

Before she'd met Falco, Yael had wondered if the Magdalene Prophecy was somehow having an effect on her and things around her — not so much the Prophecy itself as the Quickening Mary had foreseen.

The first cue had been Marco. He'd undergone a crazed transformation from what Sideris had sworn was a most-reliable secretary into the rabid creature she'd encountered in the Vat stairwell. Had it only required his tangential entanglement in the ransom demand to activate the Quickening in him?

Then there was Doctor J. What little Yael knew came from what Susan had written about him in her condolence letter to Sanford Flemming. He'd apparently suffered an uncommon form of senility that left him largely swimming in his own thoughts. Yet he'd come alive when the subject turned to the Dead Sea Scrolls, of which the Magdalene Prophecy was the lone codex.

The very same thing had happened with Falco. His fugue had only lifted with the mention of the Magdalene Treasure.

If the Quickening was real, then both J and Francesco were sure victims.

And how could Yael overlook the incredible storm that had diverted her Marseilles-Rome flight to Sardinia?

Was it just a freak phenomenon that coincidentally created a flightpath leading only to Olbia? Not likely. What else could it be but the Quickening?

It was as if Yael had been guided *away* from Rome. As if the Quickening knew that being there would serve no purpose. That being with Thomas *would*.

But why and to what end?

Not that the crossing from Sardinia to Maddalena had been a cakewalk. Anything but! And this is where things got interesting for Yael. She'd not really thought about it before. But what *on Earth* had compelled her to take such a risk crossing the sea with so much to caution against it?

The most obvious warning had been the weather itself, which she'd witnessed from the air. Then came the cabbie who'd taken her to the ferry port — then the dock-master himself.

There was no question that it had been Yael's own inner drive that brought her to Thomas's small island. But wherefrom *that* impulse? The choice had been reckless and completely uncharacteristic of her.

She'd been mid-assignment with a fast-closing deadline and extraordinary circumstances. Yet the thought of *risk* hadn't even crossed her mind. Why? And what a risk she'd taken! The effort was akin to parting waters in order to save herself and Tritone from being lost at sea.

Then in Maddalena when she and Thomas had been driving to his house through the growing storm, he'd stopped at the park. They'd been looking at one of the town's statues when another massive strike had blasted. The tip of the lightning had touched the statue itself! Right where they'd been looking!

If it too had been the Quickening, then what purpose had it served? What was it telling her?

She'd seen the statue before with children climbing all over. It was a bronze horse pulling a chariot. But this time there had been no children. Instead, white-feathered birds had adorned it, making it look like Pegasus.

Was there a message in that? Was it meant to represent Yael taking flight? Ascending above the pains of her past?

Was it possible the Quickening operated on two levels? The Outer as well as the Inner?

The outer effects would have caused the storm and the lightning strikes. The inner ones would have affected her motivations and choices — and surfaced feelings and memories she'd long kept buried.

And was it possible the Quickening was summoning a release and a transformation? *A healing?* This was not a concept that Yael was comfortable with. But she couldn't deny the possibility, given the experience she was having.

At the age of seventeen, Yael had cast herself in the mold of a Perfect Warrior. She'd fixed herself sturdily in that image. But then she'd met Thomas. And a lot had happened with him.

She'd spoken about things from her past. *Painful* things from her past. Things she *never* spoke of.

Thomas had aroused emotions in her like he'd woken a bear in hibernation for decades. She'd opened her soul to him. The sadness. The casualties of her childhood. All of the grief and despair.

In the span of mere days her great dam had burst.

And then after she'd learned the supposed fate of the Treasure from Falco, she'd been with Thomas when another Quickening had struck in their midst. Had it been signaling her that the hunt for the Treasure wasn't yet over?

Yael now knew the truth. The Treasure had *not* in fact been destroyed in the failed exchange. The Magdalene Prophecy had *not* been rendered null and unfulfilled.

And possibly—if the fates *were* guiding a greater unfolding—*just possibly...*, Yael was drawing near.

Just possibly, Yael was chancing on destiny.

CHAPTER 21

*a*s Yael ran along the manicured lawns of Piedmont Park, her thoughts were interrupted by a *patter* of colors. A butterfly with a vibrant tiger pattern crossed in front of her path. She slowed and followed it's lilted flutterings against the great soft blue expanse of the sky.

Suddenly she could hear her voice inside her own head. It was a recitation of the Gospel of J, an echo of the words she'd read when she first discovered it on Marco's phone. It was the part that captured the very essence and began with Jesus speaking to Mary Magdalene about what had transpired in the years since His Ascension.

Their teachings around sin, crucifixion, resurrection and ascension; compassion, forgiveness, healing and love had become riddled to distortion by the limited beliefs of those who had never truly grasped what they had come to reveal. And much more would soon be lost through the vagaries of time. Such was the consequence of the hapless flaws of misperception, the stony resistance of disbelief.

He beseeched Mary to preserve the unadulterated truth of what they'd taught in her precious words. For none other than she had embodied it so completely.

Then Jesus magically brought forth a dazzling spherical crystal in front of His chest. This Sacred Orb, as He called it, would bring untold power to whomever possessed it. All of Mary's senses were overwhelmed. And she wept as Jesus placed it into her outstretched hands.

Jesus guided Mary to conceal the Sacred Orb and her precious words separately in the world where they would remain in obscurity for generations to come.

And then He took Mary's face in His hands and kissed her lips. An incredible surge of energy like the force of an infinite waterfall cascading from heaven coursed through her body. She was one with the light of all truth. Her palms and fingertips began to vibrate and she knew this to be a sign it was now time to scribe the wisdom.

And so it was to be fulfilled. The immaculate teachings recorded by Mary. Her precious words to be written upon papyrus and bound in a codex that would come to be known as the Magdalene Prophecy.

Once Jesus's presence had faded, Mary experienced a second vision, this one foretold of the future. She foresaw a time when the darkness of the past would give way to a more enlightened world. When the misperceptions of old would be brought into the light and made whole.

This would be the time of the Reckoning. The Magdalene Prophecy would emerge from a holy grail. The Sacred Orb freed from its petrified shell. Together they would be given into the hands of a man and a woman chosen to bring forth the seeds of greater understanding.

She wrote,

We fulfill our promise in the Sacred Orb and my precious words inscribed on these pages. Indeed these are the Most Treasured of Treasures.

Our Treasure shall find its way into the hands of the Two who are as One. Man and woman. Equal unto each other. Whole each and as one.

From the twisted limbs of the aged olive shall come a sunlit world given in entirety, absent the shadows of earthly ignorance.

Rejoice in the celestial music of this new world for it sings of our promise.

When the shell of disbelief is broken in the world, it shall be a sign that the era of resistance is overcome. Those with eyes to see shall know that this marks the end of the era of faith and the beginning of the era of love.

We caution you, be watchful. Worldly distractions would keep you from it. Set your sights beyond the stars and my Sacred Orb shall be found. As above, so below.

Know that the Two who are as One in possession of our Treasure shall inherit infinite power over the world. For to those who are chosen, much will be given. They shall have everlasting life, abundance, peace and joy. Indeed they shall acquire a love surpassing any the world has yet known.

Our Treasure shall reveal that which most men would deny, for we have conveyed the light of our understanding unto them that they may in time stir mankind to the truth of their purpose in being.

All who chance upon our Treasure will forever be changed.

Those who seek to unlock our mysteries shall face a perilous journey indeed. For they shall know death before knowing life again. If even so fortunate. If even so brave.

For all with ears to hear, know my love shall return and come unto you when you and your beloved in oneness are ready.

The Two who are as One shall be guided by this our Treasure through the sands of all time to prepare mankind for the Second Coming of Christ. Once all is made ready, He shall emerge. The Christ from your midst. From the darkness into the light. He will have been birthed in the womb of one who is chosen. And He shall come forth from a secret and hidden thread which has spanned all of time. His name shall be Afti. And He shall have the radiant face of grace.

So shall it be.

CHAPTER 22

*I*t took a moment for Yael to recover from the magical spell she'd been under.

The tiger-skin butterfly was flitting further into the blue with the unique airy playfulness known for its kin. Yael now picked up her pace with that same playful ease. As she ran, her thoughts returned to Thomas.

He was unlike any man she'd ever known. Not that she'd known many very well. It wasn't her habit to allow for much intimacy beyond a quick roll in the sack. In that regard, Thomas was different. He was her first— The first that she'd let in.

Initially, Yael had been restless in Maddalena. But it didn't take long before she found herself slowing her rhythm. She'd always had a habit of waking with dawn's break. But in Thomas's home, she was sleeping peacefully, snuggled in the warmth of his bed well into the morning, while he rowed his kayak up and down the western shoreline.

He treated her like a princess, and she felt beautiful. She felt loved. Not since the faded memory of what her mother had been could she remember feeling this way. Somehow, Falco too had kindled this tenderness in her. But with Thomas, there was more. It was as if he was in full acceptance of exactly who she was. Scars, wounds and all.

This was much more than even Yael gave herself. She had always felt that her fate was a dark one. As if there were unseen forces at play directing her life. As if anything better wasn't even a choice.

Her only understanding of anything different came from the old feel-good movies she'd seen as a girl in that hell-house of a foster home. She'd always imagined that *feel-good* was the norm that escaped her. And so Yael had come to believe as a child that the pictures she was watching were taunting her, mere silver screened patina inspiring false hope for the *hopeless* infection inside her.

From her mother's suicide to the hellish foster home, the lonely boarding school and the horror of Wagu. Even the unknowable Ben Saba. Her life had run its own sorry course.

Yael was caught between Pinocchio and the gingerbread-man. All three of them just dying to be real.

She and Thomas hadn't talked about what this was — this *thing* going on between them. Or where it might go. But as far as Yael was concerned, it could go on forever.

Yael's diaphragm spasmed. She broke her stride for a beat and drew in one deep breath. After a second and a third, she returned to her gait.

To be perfectly candid, this wasn't the sum of her truth. She held suspicions about Thomas that still lingered. After all, it was *his* statue that perfectly matched the seal on the ransom envelope. And the description he'd given of his dealings with Harry Chudnow was strange. Almost too strange to be true. Or perhaps too strange *not* to be true.

It had left Yael questioning Thomas. Could he have sent the ransom letter? Might he be her new mark? But of course, that made no sense. Thomas wouldn't have needed to mail the envelope from the United States. Nor would he have needed to volunteer information to Yael—*any* information—about Chudnow, which surely he would not have done if he was somehow involved.

Besides, Tech's background check showed Thomas had enjoyed a successful career as an architect. He'd designed numerous projects throughout Europe. His last had been in The Algarve, Portugal, a large multi-use residential-commercial land development in which he'd had a stake. This is where he'd made the lion's share of his wealth. He was officially retired, though he continued to develop projects privately.

No. Writing Thomas into the crime was nonsensical. It was forcing a connection to the Magdalene Treasure that just wasn't there. And yet suspicious she'd been. Even though not one of her suspicions had panned out. Not yet, at least.

Yael gasped. And there was the rub. Right there in her words. *Not yet...*

CHAPTER 23

*Y*ael slowed to a jog until she came to rest in front of a pond peppered with ducks. She took in the idyllic stillness of the water as her breathing gently eased.

It was a beautiful day, and the air was sweet with the fragrant humidity of the South. Yael bent low and stretched out her calves.

She was facing a lifetime of habit-forming that caused her to doubt. To keep men at a distance— Men and women both. She'd had a lifetime of trusting no one. And it would take a leap of faith to move beyond this. To once and for all set aside her suspicious nature.

A part of her was drawn powerfully to Thomas. This much was undeniable. But she had no idea what to make of it. No idea at all.

A tiny duckling feather drifted into sight. She remembered how she'd once been so excited to dress up in a frilly gown, and at that moment the clear memory came into her mind. As her mother placed a tiara on Yael's head she heard the words again, as if for the first time. *You are a real live princess, my love. And one day you'll meet your prince.*

Out of the blue, verses from the Gospel of J floated into her mind.

We fulfill our promise in the Sacred Orb and my precious words inscribed on these pages. Indeed these are the Most Treasured of Treasures.

Our Treasure shall find its way into the hands of the Two who are as One. Man and woman. Equal unto each other. Whole each and as one.

Yael hadn't really thought about what might have happened had Bonnie & Carlo *not* died. The fact of the matter was the Treasure had found its way into their hands. It was not such a stretch to think that they might actually have been the *intended* Two As One.

But Bonnie & Carlo hadn't survived. Had their deaths created a vacancy yet to be filled?

The rightful heirs to the Treasure were described as, *Two who are as One. Man and woman. Equal unto each other. Whole each and as one.*

Was it possible that she, Yael, was now rising to become one of those two that Mary had prophesied two thousand years ago?

If so, it meant that there was another who would join her. The second of two.

Suddenly, the sun bounced off the surface of the pond, and Yael caught a glimpse of her mother's sparkling eyes. A stream of chills swept through her. The feeling was electric. More than electric. It was powerful — a seeming pulse of love. And it filled Yael with a sense of greatness no warrior training could equal.

Was Thomas her prince? Were they the Two As One destined to receive the Most Treasured of Treasures, destined to fulfill the Magdalene Prophecy?

And it was at that moment that Yael knew nothing in her life would ever be the same.

The Most Treasured of Treasures. The words echoed mystically in the cloudless expanse of her inner blue sky.

CHAPTER 24

*Y*ael sat in a quiet corner of the St. Regis hotel lounge in the chic Atlanta neighborhood of Buckhead and reviewed her day. The USPS had proved to be a difficult organization to get information from. Yael could blame stupidity, but it was more likely she'd simply received a lesson in the imperturbable national security put in place by the America-of-late.

She'd just burned a cross-Atlantic trip failing to accomplish something that Tech would have handled with ease. Perhaps it was time to shift her stance on his involvement.

Tech had been her find. Not Ben's. And she'd never discussed one with the other. There had never been a conflict, and she would have to trust that wouldn't change now.

She wasn't about to risk turning on her work phone again, not with all that was at stake. She didn't want to risk alerting Ben to her whereabouts or activities. Better to stay in the shadows and off the radar. After all, the Treasure was ripe for the taking.

Yael made sure the VPN was activated on her personal mobile phone. It would ensure an untraceable internet connection. Then she opened the VOIP App which accessed an internet phone line. She hit some buttons and waited for the telltale click.

"Tech," announced an artificial voice.

"It's Yael. I have—"

"I don't recognize your number," his tinny voice cut in.

"It's me," said Yael.

"You need to connect with me through my App."

"You've taken my calls before," she persisted.

"From the number I know."

"I can't," she said.

"Why?"

"I can't," she repeated. "This is my personal phone."

Tech said nothing.

Yael took the silence as an opportunity to inform him about her discovery of the USPS courier envelope. She told him what she'd been through at the Dead Letter Office and then provided him with a screenshot of the waybill.

"Find everything you can about the original sender of the ransom envelope," she said.

Tech hesitated only a second before acquiescing. "Fine," he said.

"I also want a video enhanced," said Yael.

"What is it?"

"An old VCR recording. It's not the greatest quality."

"How old?"

"1973."

"What's it of?"

"Standard security surveillance."

She could have been talking to a robot if not for the synthesized sound of Tech's breathing. He was thinking. There was also the faint sound of keys being tapped in the background.

"Do you have a VCR player hooked up to a television?"

"I have one better. The video has been digitized on an SD card."

"That should be enough to work with. I've got just the tool."

"I need a super clear video."

"I understand. I won't know for certain until I see it. But if we're lucky, I can fill in missing data bits. We'll end up with digital images that eclipse the quality of the original tape and come close to modern recording quality."

"I need it quickly," said Yael.

"That will be a problem," said Tech matter-of-factly. "This is a complicated process. It takes time."

"Fine. Do what you can. I'll send you a link to download from the cloud. Start with the pregnant woman in a wheelchair. Do your best to identify her. If that doesn't work, then focus on all the women entering the Vatican that morning before her departure. Try and find a match."

CHAPTER 25

*W*hile Tech got busy working his magic, Yael thought about the ransom letter. Even though it had been written almost fifty years before, the sender was presumably utilizing it to effect his ransom today.

She took it out of her bag and started reading in the hope that something would pop.

Cardinal Sideris,

Your Eminence,

We know about the great secret you have held so dearly. The secret of an ancient bronze globe and your precious codex, the Magdalene Prophecy.

We know they had once been centuries hidden beneath your hallowed spaces and concealed by you, unbeknownst to the world, unbeknownst even to your ascendant kin.

Unbeknownst to the world, unbeknownst even to your ascendant kin. Yael had glanced over this before. She now wondered what it meant.

The Globe had only just been discovered before its theft. But the Codex...

Was the Sideris of 1973, Adolfos Sideris, the only one who knew about it? Could it be that not even the others in the Church were aware of its existence?

And if this was true, it brought meaning to the line in the first paragraph — *your precious Codex*. According to Falco, prior to the theft, the Codex had been held in the Vatican's Hidden Archives. The Archives that only Adolfos Sideris was privy to. As if it was his own personal cache.

Yael turned back to the letter.

Your Eminence, we write to you of their theft. From your Vatican grasp the Magdalene Treasure was taken and now rests in ours.

The Gospel of J is astounding! Such great secrets you keep.

Secrets of a prophecy scribed by the hand of Mary Magdalene.

Secrets of her vision of a Sacred Orb (or shall we say the Sacred Bronze Globe!) brought forth to herald the Second Coming of Christ.

Such wondrous secrets!

We know too of your other secrets, Your Eminence. Such threatening secrets! Secrets you hold which might topple your Church. We ponder, to whom are the loyalties that bind you?

While Yael had learned about *Panos* Sideris's other secrets—hidden wealth, a secret family and a pipeline of tens of millions flowing through his accounts—she didn't know enough about *Adolfos* Sideris. But somehow, Bonnie & Carlo clearly did.

Yael could remember Falco disparaging the man. He'd called him a stooge and said he wasn't even a Cardinal. But those were mere expressions of disdain. At least that's how she'd taken it at the time.

Falco had told her that he'd handled some delicate matters for Sideris and the Vatican in the past, which is what led to his involvement in the theft of the Magdalene Treasure. The Cardinal's trust in

Falco was strong enough that he'd given him full authority to handle the affair. And when things had turned sour with the ransom conditions, Sideris had given Falco access to the full sum of one hundred million dollars to use at his discretion.

Yael ran through Falco's retelling of the events of '73 to see if she could recall what else she'd learned about Sideris the First. There wasn't really anything of any significance. He was killed on the night of December 25th — and his family soon after. He'd known Carlo long before the theft and was shocked to learn that Carlo was the thief.

He had tremendous clout at the Vatican and had managed to get his way despite the objections of a bickering College of Cardinals. And his clout extended beyond the Vatican walls as well. What had Falco said? Something to the tune of, *Not everyone knew how much power he wielded.*

As Yael considered this now, she realized she'd missed the opportunity to pursue the subject of Adolfos Sideris further with Falco. Now it was too late. The old man was too far gone.

Nevertheless, the significant point Bonnie & Carlo had made in the letter was that whatever Adolfos's *other* secrets were, they were big enough to topple the Church. And they were clearly referring to secrets *other than* the secret of the Magdalene Treasure.

There was one more thing to be gleaned from that last bit of the letter — one word that just couldn't be missed. Bonnie & Carlo had queried, *To whom are the LOYALTIES that bind you?*

Yael was all too familiar with the term yet knew not the full scope of its meaning. Ben Saba, himself, had instructed her, *Panos Sideris is a Loyal. Treat him as such.*

This was a puzzle all its own, one she'd just have to decode another time.

CHAPTER 26

 ael continued to the next line of the ransom letter.

Your Eminence, we may be brought to appreciate how we might benefit in returning these objects to you. It would not take much to convince us.

We sense it would be most grievous should they fall into hands other than yours. We would not wish to cause you such torment.

Again this underscored the risk to the Cardinal of losing the Treasure. The question remained, was it just to protect the Church or was there possibly more at stake?

Forgive our boldness, Your Eminence, but should you seek the return of the Sacred Bronze Globe and the Magdalene Prophecy, you will prepare to exchange one hundred million dollars.

This was clearly a ruse that had been designed by Bonnie & Carlo to *offer* an exchange for the sheer purpose of effecting an escape from which they'd never be pursued. Put simply, from the very start they'd set out to get away with the Treasure as well as ten million dollars.

And it probably would have worked if not for the accidental explosion of their van.

You will signal your readiness by the release of smoke from the Sistine Chapel. Our eyes will be trained to the chimney at 15:30 on each day henceforth. You have until the day before our wondrous night light next fades — which is the date we now set for the exchange we shall make.

Time is of the essence, Your Eminence. Once the great, soft light disappears, so shall the Magdalene Treasure, forevermore from your grasp.

This was the curious part. Had today's ransomer, Bonnie or Carlo or whoever else it might be, intended to follow the same timeline? And what did that mean if they did? It was too late to tell. The delay caused by the hold-up in the Dead Letter Office made that a certainty.

We ardently await your signal.

"Yours truly, Bonnie & Carlo," Yael said out loud to herself, signing the letter with the names it omitted.

The review hadn't uncovered anything new that would help her today. Only more questions. But it did remind her that there was a great deal on the line. Far more than a hundred million dollars.

At stake were the Prophecy itself and all it foretold. The Second Coming, the Quickening, the very fate of humanity hung in the balance.

Yael's thoughts were broken by the flash of her phone. She picked up the call before it could ring.

Tech's metallic voice broke through. "There's not much in the Dead Letter Office's systems about the sender of the ransom envelope. Records don't reveal the identity, but the file does trace its origin to the west coast of the country. The Leucadia Post Office on Phoebe Street in Encinitas, California. That's just north of San Diego."

Finally a meaningful lead. Yael couldn't be sure her mark was there. He could be anywhere in Encinitas or anywhere in California for all that mattered. He might have simply passed through and used Leucadia as a launching point for his ransom demand. Nonetheless, it was the best place for her to start.

Yael was at least two weeks behind where she would have been had she not overlooked the courier envelope sent by the DLO in Marco's satchel. And yet what she'd gained in the meantime seemed much more valuable. Independence from Ben.

He'd closed his file. The Treasure was now hers alone to pursue.

"Begin a search of the area for any connection to similar crimes. You know what to look for."

"How extensive a search?"

"Until you find me something."

"I'll start with Leucadia and sweep out from there."

CHAPTER 27

*I*t was the middle of a star-speckled night in Leucadia. The New Moon hid herself behind a cloak of secrecy as she hung unseen over the shadowed sands of the coastline that held her namesake, Moonlight Beach.

A now-short splayed-wax candle still flamed brightly in a bedroom window of one of the cliffside homes overlooking the sea. The young raven-haired woman inside had been tossing and turning for hours amidst a tangle of twisted sheets and blankets. She yearned for the moment when her thoughts would not be drowned by the mighty waves of sadness and grief that death left in its wake.

At last, a somnolent blanket overcame her as if some silent lullaby was soothing her. And Isabelle Merchant dropped into sleep.

She was carried to a warm beach at sunset, just a child, not more than three. Playing in the shallow surf. In her tiny hands was a starfish.

"Look Mummy!" she squealed and ran.

Marie crouched in the soft sand to catch her daughter.

"A starfish! Wow! Isn't she beautiful?"

Tucking her daughter in the nook of bent legs, Marie pointed to each of the creature's slow-moving arms in her child's gentle clasp and counted. Isabelle sang along.

"Can I take her home Mummy?"

"Oh… Isa, the starfish already has a home. Swimming with her family in the sea," she consoled, her eyes shining brightly.

"Nooo, Mummy!" Isa raised the starfish to her lips and in a breathy whisper begged, "I really want you to come home with me. I love you starfish."

"Isa, my love, I'm sure she is happy to have met you. And to have spent a little time with you. But now I think she'd like to go home. Before it gets dark."

Marie gently caressed Isabelle's hair, then rose and carried her to the surf, cradling her child's back against her own chest so that her child was floating on air.

"Come. Let's help her swim home. Wait for the next big wave to come in, then set her down so she can swim out with the tide."

They crouched quietly as many big waves swept in. Marie's patience was undying. Minutes passed in silence while Isabelle sat fascinated by the creature.

"Now Mummy?"

"Yes, my love."

Isabelle watched as the starfish slowly disappeared with the surf. Her mother cradled her. The waves washed quietly through their toes and away and through them and away. The waters glistened like diamonds as the sun began its slip over the distant edge.

Isabelle turned suddenly and leaned into her mother. They both tumbled backward, their faces inches apart. Isabelle sparkled as she brought her nose to her mother's playfully and stared into her eyes.

"Eskimo kiss!" she squealed and pressed their faces together.

They laughed and kissed, and Marie held her child close to her breast. It was one of those precious moments of pure love that births echoes in time and space.

"I love you, Mummy."

"I love you too, my sweet."

"How much do you love me, Mummy?"

"This much!" Marie stretched her arms as wide as she could, feigning exertion.

"That's all?" Isabelle's face danced with mischief.

Her mother's eyes sparkled as she pointed to the pale orb climbing in the east. "Isa, I love you all the way to the moon and back."

Isabelle gazed at that magic lantern in the sky, imagining how much love there could be between her and the moon. *So, so much!*

And as she stood mesmerized, cradled by her mother's love, the moon became a golden disk hanging right before her. She melted into its brilliance as flashes of white, blue, red and green appeared on its surface — stars dancing on a sea of gold! Dance with us, they seemed to be singing. Dance!

"Remember this," the soft voice of her mother echoed through the fogs of sleep. "Remember."

Isabelle awoke no more a child and remembered. The dream still clear in her mind, even clearer in her heart.

Tears filled her eyes as she breathed deeply, inhaling her mother's embrace, her salty-sweet breath, and her lovely, loving voice.

Out through the window of her cliffside bedroom in the distant dark of night above the unseeable sea, the moon hung unlit. She could swear its faint presence was still speckled and its speckles still beckoned, ever playfully, her new moon slowly dancing full.

CHAPTER 28

The next morning Isabelle arose early from another restless night. She was exhausted right down to her bones. It felt like the weeks of sleeplessness were cascading toward an avalanche.

Isa decided she wouldn't risk battling sleep in her bedroom another night. So she tucked a small bag into the trunk of her little black roadster, dropped the top and took off. She was headed through the desert to a place her mother absolutely loved. It was a full day's drive away, but she'd break it up with a visit to a watering hole she'd discovered with her college friends a decade ago.

An hour later, Isabelle parked on a familiar sun-baked lane that looked like it went nowhere. The sun was high in the eastern horizon, and she spotted a speck moving quickly through the blue. It left a perfect stream in its wake.

Isa loved the skies. She'd dreamt of flying as a child, and when she was old enough she'd earned her wings as a private pilot.

She didn't get up in the clouds quite often enough. If she'd planned this trip, it would have been the perfect moment to pilot a plane, to escape to the freedom of the lower heavens. But there'd been no planning. Only an early morning impulse.

She looked down at the baked clay at her feet. Just as well. This was a beautiful spot. Isa grabbed her daypack and set off on foot through the dry desert scrub.

For the last two weeks, memories of Marie had swarmed her like the piercing drone of grievous wasps. She'd taken that time to remember her mother, saying aloud the few things she'd left unsaid. And when her thoughts had surfaced all the petty wrongs from their lifetime together, Isa begged forgiveness.

Now the memories still buzzed, but they were more akin to a charm of hummingbirds beckoning her to remember. *Remember it all.*

Isa eventually found the small trail she knew would be there and followed it through the chaparral as she climbed the soft hills of the Laguna Mountains. She huffed up the first, surprised by how steep it was and how much her legs ached at the top. But then she dutifully trekked the dirt path as it wound through the brush and took her down the far slope. She continued until she came to the face of another towering rise and a creek coursing its way through the valley.

She cocked her head to listen for the sound of crashing water but all she could hear was the chirping of crickets, the scuttle of lizards and the soft desert wind. Upstream was her goal, and after trekking an hour, Isa reached it.

It was not the cascading waters alone that were magical. It was the sum total stretched out before her. She had walked into a lush oasis that opened to the sky. A majestic waterfall was set against a backdrop of granite. And at its base a beautiful pool of cobalt blue.

Alone in her sanctum, Isa stripped off her clothes and plunged into the water. It was deliciously cool, though not as cold as she'd thought. The heat of the desert left nothing untouched. She played in the pond, glad that the higher mountains were set back far enough for the late-morning sun to brighten this spot.

After a while, she lifted herself onto a large boulder which sat like an island in the heart of the pool. There she lay and basked in the heat of the sunshine.

The spray from the falls sprinkled mist on her skin, while the hypnotic spell melodiously lulled her to a deep calm. Before long, her own memories cascaded.

~

*I*sa's mother Marie had studied to be a Montessori Director in order to have a career that kept her close to her child. And so Isa had grown up in Marie's small school first as a student and in time as her mother's young aide. It was no surprise to anyone that she one day chose to become a teacher herself.

Soon after Isa joined her mother at the helm, they constructed a new schoolhouse on an idyllic property in the crown jewel of San Diego, the town of La Jolla. This was accomplished with the help of a wealthy parent who believed in them both.

Their new schoolhouse had filled quickly. Isa loved every one of the precious children. She loved the school. She loved their team.

But more than all these, she loved her mother.

Marie had been feeling unwell for a couple of weeks. It started as a pain in her ribs.

"Nothing broken. Nothing torn," her doctor said after examining the x-rays. "I wouldn't worry. It's a tiny fracture at best. Not uncommon. Nothing to be done except avoid exertion. Give it time to mend."

An over-the-counter pain reliever helped a bit until someone told Isa about a miracle sports gel at the dollar store. Isa would sit beside Marie as she lay in her bed and rub the gel wherever there was pain. She would then place her hands on Marie's body and think only of the love she felt for her mother. Isa had once studied Reiki and believed that a healing force could move through her hands.

It was effective for a while. But Isa was saddened when Marie no longer found relief from these efforts. The pain had worsened. What was confounding to all was that it would shift. While it was pretty consistently in that same place in her lower left ribs, sometimes the pain would be in her belly, at other times to the far right of her belly.

For Isa, this was extremely upsetting. Watching her mother suffer in this way left her feeling helpless. Isa had always seen her mother handle everything with such grace. And this was no different.

Marie wouldn't complain unless asked. Or unless things were so bad that tears would drown her face. Even then, she would weep quietly and fall into the cradle of Isa's arms.

Isa wanted nothing more than to put an end to her mother's suffering. She spent all of her time with her, knowing in her heart how much comfort this brought. And there was nothing more important than that. The pair loved each other's company, had always done so. But this was different. Something deep was tugging at Isa, and she just couldn't stand to be apart.

Her doctor ordered an MRI. Isa contracted a private clinic and had it performed the very next day. Nothing was found other than two tiny, age-related lesions on her liver. Nothing that would explain the pain.

Then unexpectedly one day, light appeared in their tunnel. Relief at last! Marie's doctor decided to try something new and prescribed some pills for neural pain. The results were amazing. Marie felt immediately better, her pain quickly at bay.

Unfortunately, Fibromyalgia was diagnosed. The neural disorder was not completely understood, but it was at least known to involve the misfiring of neurons that created ghost symptoms of pain where there otherwise would be none. It explained why Marie could never pinpoint one single source of the aches in her belly.

After what had been a period of ever-increasing torment, finally, she could breathe. Managing the pain, however, was an extremely delicate exercise. Nonetheless, life had brightened for them both.

Isa and Marie went for long drives, enjoyed ice cream and took short walks on the beach. Although Marie still ate very little, they visited all of her favorite restaurants. It was a time for celebration.

Marie had wanted to visit their schoolhouse often. She would go from classroom to classroom, gently interrupting the activities to share treats from the market.

The children adored Marie. She cuddled and kissed them and listened to their every word as if they were little angels from above.

She would gather them in a circle on the floor and read stories, often creating her own in the moment, exaggerating events from her own life and enriching them with fantasy and a childlike perspective. It reminded Isa of the same magical affection she'd received as a child.

It was on such a day that Marie stepped into one of the classrooms to share snacks and tall tales. Isa stood outside the room peeking in through the one-way glass designed for unobtrusive observation. She could see the children giggling and squealing and plucking grapes as Marie lit them all up with her love.

Unfortunately, Marie's meds had been left at home that day, and the exertion caused her pain to sweep in terribly fast. By the time Isa rushed Marie back to her home, she was bowled over in pain. It took three full doses before the fire in her belly finally subsided.

Nothing could have prepared Isa for what came the following week. Results from an ultrasound found the definitive source of Marie's torment. A massive tumor had been found.

"It's terminal," said the doctor. "Six months, a year at most."

Isa froze.

Marie sat quietly for a moment then turned to her doctor. "Thank you," she said and kissed his cheek.

It was a kiss of gratitude, not much unlike how Jesus had kissed Judas for having set his destiny in motion. It was a powerful moment that Isa would never forget, a testament to the woman her mother truly was.

For Isa, the news was an axe to the side of the head. She couldn't even say the name of the disease out loud, like doing so would summon the devil. This form of cancer was notoriously hard to diagnose, and it was most often too late by the time it was found.

Such was the case with Marie.

$\mathcal{M}$arie's disease progressed quickly from this point forth. It was excruciating for Isa to watch as her beautiful mother's body lost its vitality, becoming weaker and thinner with each passing day.

Marie, in turn, had no choice but to surrender to the course her life had taken. She did so with all the grace and inner-strength with which she had done all things in life.

Isa rarely left her side. She'd only skip out to run errands when Marie was sleeping. One afternoon, a neighbor came by with some cake.

"You look exhausted Isa," she said. "Go upstairs and nap for a couple of hours. I'll be here."

Isa heard the tumble through the muffle of sleep. It was dark outside. *What was it she'd heard?* Then, a soft whimpering.

No!

The neighbor had gone. It was the most horrible feeling in all the world to find Marie in a crumpled heap at the bottom of the tight spiral steps she adored so much. There she lay, wrenched in pain, unable even to lift herself up.

Isa cradled her mother and carefully, gently lifted her from the ground and, bearing as much of her mother's weight as she could, slowly walked her up to her bedroom.

It wasn't even a week before Isa's exhaustion took over again. She tucked her mother into bed and at Marie's insistence went to sleep early. This time Isa was awoken by a shriek. It took her a while to register where she was. Then her mother's voice called out in desperation.

By the time Isa ran to her mother's side, she'd been hanging for a few minutes, clinging to the staircase rails to keep from falling further down the steps. A cup of tea had spilt everywhere.

Isa crouched at her mother's side. But the horror and shock of seeing Marie in this way overcame her and all Isa could do was bury her face and sob. At last, with pain written all over her face, Marie whispered hoarsely, "Please lift me up."

It was a few breaths before Isa was able to collect herself enough to carry her weakened mother up into her room and provide her the injections she so desperately needed.

Once Marie finally fell asleep, Isa washed the staircase carpet as best she could and laundered her mother's tea-stained housecoat. Then she set her alarms, so she'd be ready to inject the medicines her mother would need to get through the night.

It was a long while before Isa broke the sobs that shook her that night. Nothing could quell the sadness and guilt she felt for not having been there to prevent her mother's fall, for having left her alone just so she could get some sleep.

She turned to the heavens as if to cry.

What are you doing to the Queen of my world?!

Isa dozed on the floor alongside Marie's bed. She wanted to be there when her mother woke up in the morning. She wanted to beg forgiveness.

When morning light came, Marie roused first and was looking down at Isa when she awoke.

"Thank you for taking care of me," Marie said before Isa could rub the sleep from her eyes. "Thank you for loving me."

"Mum…," Isa started, then broke into sobs, unable to speak.

"Forgive me," Marie continued, "For all the pain and difficulty I'm causing you. Forgive me for anything I've *ever* done to hurt you, Isa. You are so precious to me. You are my jewel. The light of my life. Please forgive me."

"No," Isa said, as regret shook her bones.

But Marie interrupted, knowing her thoughts. "Isa, you've done nothing wrong. You're so brave and strong. I couldn't do this without you. And my love, I want you to be at peace.

"Open this drawer," she said, pointing to her bedside. "There. My pendant."

Isa pulled out her mother's precious jewelry from where it had been placed each night before bed for as long as she could remember. Isa had never known Marie not to wear it, except when she'd been sleeping. Even when a formal gown called for something more delicate. Even at the beach.

"Please put it on," Marie said in a whisper, her voice breaking. "Now it's yours. Wear it as I've done. And promise me one day you'll give it to your daughter."

Isa's eyes burst in a flood. She knew what this meant. Marie was truly letting go. Isa dropped her head onto her mother's breast and sobbed, unable to hold the full force of the sadness she'd been braving.

When the storm passed, Isa's cheek was still resting on her mother's chest.

"There's another one like it," Marie managed to say, before choking on her words.

The emotions overcame her and flowed silent tears into her pillow. It was not the first time she'd come close to telling Isa the story behind this pendant. But each time, sadness had come in the way.

It was obvious to Isa that Marie's memories were too painful to remember. So she didn't ask. Instead, she just lay there, her heart breaking at seeing her mother this way. Such a precious soul. Yet still so much pain.

Marie's voice poked through, "I want to stay here in my home. Until my time comes."

Isa choked back more sorrow and nodded.

"Don't be afraid," Marie said as she closed her eyes, "I'm not."

And then she slept.

Within a few days, Marie's pain had increased exponentially. A palliative care nurse, Wendy Lea, an exemplar of the goodness of humanity, had been brought in to provide support through the night. It allowed Isa the time she needed to sleep and recharge. Other nurses came intermittently throughout the day to check in on Marie and ensure she was comfortable.

By week's end, Marie was so deeply sedated that she could no longer speak. No longer turn in her bed. No longer open her eyes. And yet she remained conscious of everything going on around her.

She had needed to help Wendy turn her mother in bed every few hours. Isa herself could not understand why every single time this simple task would cause her to break into silent yet unstoppable sobs as she held her mother's precious, frail, withering body. Perhaps her grieving had begun.

For Isa, the horror of this all was felt like a constant throb in her heart. Yet through it all, she had still lovingly, carefully attended to any and every need that arose. She had become at once a nurse and a soldier, a friend, and a daughter. Caring, protecting, comforting, adoring.

"It won't be long," Wendy said one evening before she left.

That night Isa crouched next to Marie as she slept, staring into the beautiful face that was her mother. Isa's love overflowed, not unlike the drops that rolled down her cheeks.

She ran her fingers through her mother's hair in the very same way that Marie had done when Isa was just a girl. To her surprise, Marie suddenly opened her eyes and gazed at her daughter.

It was *love* meeting *love*. An overwhelming stream of emotion swept through Isa. And she could tell that her mother experienced the same.

Somehow, Isa knew she'd never forget the fullness of that moment — her mother's soft skin, her light breath, her unending and powerful love.

And at the very same time, she knew it was a precious moment that would far too soon become just a memory.

CHAPTER 30

The call of a wild bird roused Isa from her thoughts. She might have fallen asleep; she couldn't be sure. But when her ears made sense of the loud splash of the waterfall, she remembered where she was.

It was then that she felt her skin. Hot and tight. She'd been lying in the sun far too long, troubled by grief, unmindful of her body's growing discomfort. The sun had unabashedly borne down on Isa. It felt like a hundred bees had planted their stingers, then tarried to burrow them even deeper into the soil of her skin.

She threw herself into the coolness of the pond and shrieked for no one to hear at the pain of it all. And as she hung there in the ache of her grief, the ache of her loss and her suffering, the ache of her burning, burning skin, the thought crept forth anew.

The thought she'd thought before. The one that asked what joy could ever come of her pain.

Would the hurting ever really end? For to do so would mean she suffered the loss no more. And that could *never* happen because Marie had meant the world to Isa.

She had been her beloved queen. Her champion. Her greatest

admirer. Her constant companion. Her precious, precious mother. And now she was gone.

And at that moment a deep resolve took hold, a clarity she'd not known these past weeks. Isa lifted her beautiful, naked body onto the stones near the falls. There was a grace in her movements, a confession of fearlessness and strength. She leapt effortlessly boulder to boulder, rising determinedly up the sheer mountain wall until she landed precariously near the very top in a narrow crook between the wall and the falls.

She bent over her thigh where a tattoo of the moon and a cross shone brightly. Isa slid her fingers over top the faint landscape of scars that ran beneath as if to trace an absent memory, a flittering something that railed at the touch of the burn on her skin. A shudder of sorrow ran through her anew, a sadness not touched by the death of Marie but different. Isa knew not why or wherefrom.

Her tears poured freely, like the falls in her midst. Such a quickening of sadness and hurt from some things she knew and others she didn't.

She looked out for a moment to the oasis below. To where the falls fell upon rocks. To the pool just beyond. Her vision clouded by the grief from within, clouded too from the mist all about.

And there in the twinkling light, she stood brazenly, brokenly, bared to the birds, to the sun, to the wind and the barreling water. For at that moment they did bear witness to a delicate beauty who stood in her grief on the cusp of a fall to a thunderous end.

Isa turned now, her back to the falls, her face to the cold, dripping-wet, grey granite wall. She slid her feet slowly to the slippery edge of the rock that was her perch and craned her head up to see the source of the deluge. Tears from above washed over her face. Mere inches behind her they fell like an orchestra of angels' harp-strings.

She unclasped her necklace. The pendant hanging from its links was the gift from Marie. She studied the image etched on its face, the image she knew was St. Thomas.

Isa traced her fingers across the inscription that ringed the Apostle. They were too small to read, but she knew them by heart.

Key to the Most Treasured of Treasures

Isa didn't know what it meant. But that hardly mattered now. She raised the pendant to her lips before setting it down on the smooth rock.

She stood there a long time, her arms collapsed by her side.

When she was ready, she inched even further back until all that remained of her on the rock were the very tips of her toes.

Then Isa drew in a final breath, as deep as she could pull, and simply let go.

As if each second was split into a hundred, Isa fell slowly back from her perch. Gradually her pendulum gained in its swing.

Suddenly her toes gave one final push out from the rock. The force thrust her away from the granite wall and powerfully through the watery veil.

In the next moment, her back arched sharply into a magnificent dive, and Isa plunged neatly into the pool below.

CHAPTER 31

*Y*ael lay on the plush quilted mattress in her suite at the Atlanta St. Regis. Her lips still held the taste of the lounge's famous and excellent Bloody Mary.

Her focus was now keenly upon discovering who had sent the ransom demand. Tech had begun a complicated search. He had no leads other than a location. Leucadia, California was ground zero. Unless Tech could work some serious magic, Yael knew that locating the person would be like finding a needle in a haystack.

She was convinced the Ransomer had to be someone connected to the thieves. Carlo Rinaldi was the known entity, while Bonnie was unknown.

Yael considered what she'd learned about the woman. Bonnie had to be the person who'd stolen the Aga Khan's precious book in '68 while Carlo was in New York. Even if Yael's logic was weak, she had to focus on this possibility, which meant Bonnie had to be somehow connected to the Vatican. She was either an employee of the museum or someone with sufficient access to permit the comings-and-goings that such an endeavor would have required.

If Bonnie *was* the counterfeiter, then she was certainly a highly-skilled artist. And she would have had a deep knowledge of valuable paintings and documents. It would have made perfect sense for her to be a curator at the Vatican specializing in the conservation and restoration of papers, the very skillset Moreau had described.

Falco and Vespucci certainly wouldn't have missed such an obvious possibility. However, had they considered the possibility that Bonnie had been at the Vatican *before* 1973? Probably not. All hope wasn't lost.

The digital employee files from Falco's investigation appended records of experts and visiting scholars who'd been associated with the Vatican Museums. Yael turned to them now. She breathed a sigh of relief when she saw that the records stretched back several years. They weren't exclusive to persons present at the Vatican in '73.

Yael sifted through the electronic documents like she was going through old photo albums — or at least what she imagined it would feel like to do such a thing. She was looking only for someone who resembled Bonnie.

It wasn't really a resemblance she looked for. It wasn't the pictures alone she studied. After all, Moreau's description of Bonnie was too vague. What Yael was looking for was something, however subtle, to trigger an *Aha*.

It might be in the eyes or the posture or even the dress. Something that might convey an air of... *Bonnie-ness*. Boldness. Intelligence. Criminality. Mischievousness. Something ethereal. She wouldn't know what until she saw it.

Yael honed in on the names of those who had been attached to the museum during the time Carlo was in New York. There were dozens of files. The majority, who'd still been at the Vatican Museums in 1973, had been investigated and questioned exceptionally well by Vespucci.

The rest were people who hadn't been on Vespucci's investigative radar, people who'd been employed or peripherally involved with the museum and had left prior to the events in 1973. There were a couple of people who'd hailed from California and a couple more who'd be believably suspect if the only measure was Moreau's profile of Carlo's vixen.

But no one made Yael's senses tingle. No one stood out until she came to the file of a frequent visiting scholar from New York University.

Susan Bailey.

Yael recognized the name immediately. It was the same person who'd written to inform Sanford Flemming of Doctor J's death.

The ransom letter's Gospel of J spelled out Doctor J's involvement in the discovery of the Magdalene Prophecy. And while Susan Bailey knew Doctor J well enough to write a condolence letter to Sanford Flemming when the man had died, it wasn't clear how exactly Susan was connected to J.

Both were linked to NYU, but that's all Yael knew. She needed to find out who in fact J was in order to understand their connection and how it played into things.

Yael studied the resume of Susan Bailey enclosed in the file. Her jaw dropped open as she realized that Susan was a leading innovator in the restoration techniques of ancient Papers. In other words, Susan had the skillset to be Carlo's partner-in-crime.

It was the *Aha* she'd been hoping for.

Had Yael just found Bonnie?

CHAPTER 32

The possibility that Susan Bailey was Carlo's mysterious accomplice opened up more questions for Yael to work out.

If she was Bonnie, had Susan known about the Codex? And how much had she known? Had she somehow discovered that the Codex hadn't been lost in the fire in Israel in 1956 as J had believed, that instead it had been secured in the Vatican vaults?

Yael picked up her phone and punched in Tech's number.

"See what you can find about Susan Bailey. Anything and every-thing—" Yael scanned the record. "My information is that she was a scholar at NYU in the Sixties and Seventies specializing in Greek Antiquities and Papers, that's scrolls and codexes.

"She's somehow linked to someone called Doctor J, also from NYU. Find who that is. And see if you can find a connection between Susan and Carlo Rinaldi, the Vatican curator who stole the Magdalene Treasure in '73."

Lifting her iPad, Yael zoomed in on the black-and-white photo-graph of Susan Bailey on the Vatican files. *Was she looking at Bonnie?*

"En—"

"Tech," she cut in. "What's happening with the surveillance video?"

"It's still being reconstructed."

"Will I see faces?"

"It'll be what I promised. As sharp as modern digital images."

"How long before it's done?"

"Not more than two hours." He paused, the sound of his fingers clicking on his keyboard filled the background. "I'm into NYU's database. It doesn't go back to the early Seventies. And there's no Susan Bailey matching your description in the online records."

"Alright."

"The search in California is underway. I'll report when I have something."

"Just get me the video," Yael said and hung up.

Tech had always been paid by way of electronic trades that Yael made with the money Ben deposited in her Bank of Geneva slush fund. Tech had devised an untraceable carriage of payments using Bitcoin. While there were new programs that could now track Bitcoin transactions, Tech. had devised countermeasures that foiled the tracking software, sending false trails that ultimately led nowhere.

This would be the first time Yael had involved Tech in anything not involving Ben. There was an ample float in her slush account to finance Tech's work, but Yael would be taking a gamble. There was a chance that Ben would see the fund being depleted.

Not that Ben would know what she was up to. Tech had nothing to do with Ben — he'd been *her* hire. Ben would never know where the money had gone, only that it had gone somewhere. And then he would know that Yael was making a move on her own.

She knew it was risky, but the key was in the timing. Yael would have to get as much out of Tech as she could and hold off his payments until absolutely necessary. It wasn't as if she could stop Tech from taking the money if push came to shove—he could certainly hack his way into her account if he wanted to—but if she could get close to the Treasure first, then none of it would matter.

Susan Bailey was an especially exciting lead. After all, Yael had been dreaming about Bonnie for a while. But given what Tech had said about the inaccessibility of older records at NYU, the only way to learn more about her meant she'd have to get on a plane and examine the files in person. Her recent trip to the post office only reminded her she could easily be setting herself up for another frustrating encounter.

And what if the two women weren't the same? A trip to New York would waste time. Before Yael ventured too far, it would be better to see if Tech's mastery with the Vatican surveillance video could prove her hypothesis.

Yael zoomed in on the file photo of Susan Bailey again.

God, I hope that you're Bonnie!

CHAPTER 33

Yael brought her thoughts back to her task.

She could list several things she now knew about the sender of the ransom letter. Firstly, the person had to be related somehow to either Bonnie or Carlo. Secondly, they had set the ball rolling from Southern California.

And third, it was quite possible that they had altered their ransom efforts and moved on to another buyer. This was because weeks had gone by while the envelope lingered in the DLO and in whichever San Diego post offices it had been before that. The New Moon deadline would have passed.

This didn't bother Yael much. Her mark either still had the Treasure or knew exactly who did. In any case, she was closing in. Come hell or high water, she'd soon get her hands on the Treasure.

Yael was still waiting for Tech's reconstruction of the Vatican surveillance video in order to compare the image of Bonnie with Susan's photograph. The result would reveal whether she was headed to New York to pursue Susan Bailey or to San Diego to hunt the sender of the ransom.

If Bonnie was Susan, Yael would hone in on NYU. Anything she could learn about Susan Bailey and Doctor J would be valuable in tracking down family, friends, associates—anyone at all—who might have been the recipient of the *real* Magdalene Treasure as well as the ransom documents from the Seventies.

New York would also give her the opportunity to check out the Met, where Carlo had spent his *sabbatical* year. Although Carlo had been cleared of the theft of the Aga Khan's book in '68 because he was in NYC, it was oddly, *remotely* conceivable that he'd been exploring expanding his criminal escapades to New York.

There would be no harm in exploring the possibility. Yael would look for similar counterfeiting-thefts that could have taken place at the New York museum during the dates Carlo was there. And if they'd continued after he left, that would point strongly to Susan Bailey operating on that end of the ocean.

For now, Yael had to remain neutral. To prematurely suppose Bonnie was Susan Bailey could lead to reckless mistakes. It would be better to keep an open mind to all possibilities.

Falco had been unable to share anything about Bonnie from his experience of the failed ransom exchanges — except that she was an intrepid motorcycle-riding criminal. In Turin, at least Marion Moreau had helped Yael see that Bonnie was the counterfeiter among the pair. Which brought up an interesting question. Was Bonnie an artist first and then a thief, or was it the other way around?

Yael also wondered what kind of relationship Bonnie had with Carlo. Had Carlo been the point man? Had he been the one to identify the art because of his access? Unless Bonnie had access too, which meant they'd both fulfilled that role.

The file photo of Susan revealed a beautiful woman. Intense eyes and strong features. She had a keen look of sophistication — and intelligence. She'd make the perfect Bonnie.

Carlo would have been a good match for her. He was no slouch. His criminal resume made that much clear.

Yael's thoughts slid back to the night of the last exchange, the night when Bonnie & Carlo had died in the explosion. They'd been heading to the bridge to complete the final exchange, the Magdalene Treasure for the remaining ninety million.

Yael had already worked out in her mind what they'd intended to do on the bridge — but not their escape. What had they planned?

It was certainly possible that the explosives in the van had been intentionally rigged. Bonnie & Carlo might have engineered a remote detonator to trigger an explosion as leverage to secure their getaway, threatening to destroy the Treasure if Falco didn't provide them safe passage to leave.

And the fact that they'd staged a fake bronze in the back of the van meant that they had intended one further twist. They'd planned to trigger the blast after getting away, enabling them to escape and keep the real Treasure in addition to the hundred million dollars.

But there was a problem with this theory. Bonnie & Carlo had no way to predict Falco's response to the threat. It could very well have ended in a stalemate right there on the bridge.

Yael mused. What would she have done in their shoes? Before too long, a picture formed in her mind.

The plan had been to trigger the explosion on the bridge as a diversion for their escape. They would have repelled off the bridge to a boat on the river below, which would have been timed to appear just after the explosion.

But something had gone wrong on the way to the bridge. A critical, unexpected misstep. Something randomly accidental. A tossed cigarette. Some haphazard spark. She'd never know which. Whatever it was, before they'd even arrived at the bridge, their fate had been sealed. Their van had blown up, burning all hope to a crisp, burning them too.

And the pilot of the getaway craft? It might have been Bonnie had the van not been conspicuously en route to the bridge when it exploded. That left one conclusion. If Yael was right, it meant that Bonnie & Carlo had another partner. An invisible, last-surviving member of their crew.

Yael twisted herself off the bed and went to the window where a peach-colored sunset swept the broad landscape. But she wasn't seeing the horizon; her mind was busy in thought about the one person she knew who could fill the shoes of partner number three. The person that Yael had long-since suspected.

The elusive art dealer Harry Chudnow was still very much in play.

CHAPTER 34

*Y*ael's mobile phone rang on the bed behind her. As she turned, a name flashed on the screen.

"Thomas!" she said, surprising herself by how happy she was that he'd called.

"Hi, Yael. How are you?"

"Fine," she said, suddenly feeling nervous. What else could she say? "And you?"

"Do you have a minute?"

"Sure."

"I'll be taking a trip in a couple of days."

"Oh, okay," she said. The fact of the matter was that Yael didn't know what she should say. She was new to this and suddenly very self-conscious.

"Well, I just wanted you to know if you return while I'm gone. Just in case, I'll give you the master security code to the property," he said and read out the six-digit alpha-numeric code.

"Where are you going?" Yael said, making an effort.

"To see a dear friend. Alesi and I work together. And he's the closest thing to family I have in my life."

"Alesi?"

Thomas chuckled. "I've known him since he was a child and just always called him Alesi. His official name is Alex Elibon."

Yael's phone buzzed as some messages were received.

"How are things going with you?" said Thomas.

Another series of texts buzzed through.

"Fine. Busy right now. Let's talk when you're back."

"I won't be long. Not more than a few days, I think. But I'll let you know if that changes."

"Okay."

"I love you."

The words caught Yael off guard. *Completely* off guard. And she could feel heat rising to her face.

"I— I'll see you soon," she stammered.

Yael wasn't quite sure what she was feeling. It was an odd mix of emotions. Among them, her suspicious mind was battling to be heard. But she would not revert to her old ways. That was behind her.

In her heart, she knew she had nothing to worry about. She'd thought it through already and drawn her conclusions. And that was the end of it, once and for all.

Yael turned her attention to the new messages that had come in from Tech. He'd summarized what he'd found on Susan Bailey through the IRS, bank files and other government records.

Her last reported employer was NYU, and her listed occupation was Fine Art Conservator & Historian. Her last tax filing was in 1973 for the 1972 tax year. The last paycheque she'd cashed was dated November 15, 1973. Bank records showed all activity ceased on November 24, 1973. Her accounts had stayed dormant for years and were eventually closed. The last renewal of her driver's license and passport had been in 1969 and 1970, respectively.

Tech had also managed to find mention of a multi-million dollar trust fund granted by her parents and registered in her name. So Susan Bailey had been or *was* a woman of means. This piqued Yael's interest.

YAEL:

ANY OTHER DETAILS ON THE TRUST FUND?

TECH:

I'M WORKING ON IT. THE LAW OFFICE CLOSED IN THE FIFTIES.

YAEL:

HOW OLD WAS SHE?

TECH:

DOB JUN 13 1940

Her age fit the mold cast for Bonnie. Susan would have been 33 years old at the time of the theft, matching the loose profile Moreau had given. Secondly, Susan was a Fine Art Conservator — exactly the skillset she'd need to counterfeit the art. And finally, there was no record of her existence at any time after November 24, 1973.

The facts were circumstantial — but overwhelmingly so. Susan had gone off the radar just two days before the Magdalene Treasure was stolen. And she'd died trying to get away with it.

Yael was convinced. Susan was Bonnie.

This meant that Yael's next stop was New York, where she'd learn as much as she could about Susan while Tech worked his magic with the ransom-envelope-lead in California.

Something would click. It had to. And soon Yael would have the ransomer snared in her sights.

Yael was already settled into the St. Regis, in one of the most luxurious suites she'd enjoyed in a while. There was no need to ruin a good night. She'd head to the airport and New York City at the break of dawn.

CHAPTER 35

Sometime later, Yael was awakened by the buzz of her cellphone. Tech had remastered the surveillance video.

She brought it up on her computer tablet. The images captured Carlo's *pregnant* accomplice as she was being wheeled from the Vatican.

Tech's improvements were dramatic. The pictures were crisp and clear, just like he'd promised. Not much different than what she'd expect from today's cameras.

"That's amazing," Yael said. "How did you do it?"

"I culled from a few things that have been on my project list for a while. There's a lot of complex programming," he said. "The original resolution standards on the surveillance video are from the olden days. And each frame on the old video format captured particular images—like the woman in the wheelchair—differently on each frame, based on how she was positioned in the shot.

"My program assembles all that data as it relates to subjects within the frames, grabbing the details and interpreting them as a whole. In essence, each frame has detail embellishing it from the rest of the film."

They played it through from beginning to end. Unfortunately, the refined video revealed little new. Bonnie's belly— *No! Susan's* belly was perfectly round, and Yael could see that she held an ornate walking stick in one hand.

"I want to see her face," said Yael, wanting to compare it to Susan Bailey's photograph in the Vatican file.

"It's not visible—" said Tech.

"What?!"

"She's concealed her identity behind a scarf and sunglasses," the digitally-altered voice explained. "I haven't been through it in detail, because you wanted it fast."

"Okay," Yael said. "I'll go through it."

"We're synched. So you can play the video back and forth and zoom in and out on your screen. I'll see it on my side."

"Fine. Leave it with me," Yael said and ended the call.

Without losing a beat, she replayed the video, this time at a slower speed. One shot captured the wheelchair bouncing off a step, which had caused Susan's glasses to slip down her nose for a flash. Yael froze the frame and zoomed in until Susan's eyes and her brow were all she could see.

As she realized what the image revealed, her jaw went slack. And Yael let out a soft groan.

Bonnie wasn't Susan.

But the more Yael looked, the more she was left with the feeling she knew who this was — not Susan Bailey but someone else.

Yael flipped through the Vatican employment files. But no one stood out. It was the same with all of the other pictures she'd gathered through the course of her investigation. Nothing matched.

Yael didn't know where to navigate next. But rather than drift aimlessly, she returned to the video. She'd seen this face before, but she needed more to piece it together. Sadly, the little that the snapshot showed just wasn't enough.

She zoomed in close seeing that the woman's features were obscured by both her disguise as well as the angle of the camera. A better shot would help.

She zoomed out, this time going forward frame by frame. The screen showed the pair moving in slow motion towards the exit.

"Freeze there!" she said, anxiously, forgetting for a moment that she was alone.

Rather than reveal something about Bonnie, the frame had managed to capture the lower part of Carlo's face as it angled out of the shade of the ball cap.

Yael could clearly make out a trio of distinct beauty marks. A dark mole on his nose and two others on his cheek and his chin.

But that wasn't right! Yael flipped to the picture of Carlo in the employee file.

No moles.

It wasn't him!

What the fuck?!

Yael took a second look at the face of the man she now knew *wasn't* Carlo. The features were somewhat familiar. She'd seen him before — the same as Bonnie.

Again she turned to the Vatican files and scanned the photographs one at a time. At last, she found it. The same blemishes, in exactly the same spots. Except that the man in the file was born in 1899, which would have made him seventy-four in '73. While the man pushing the wheelchair in the video was clearly a spry forty years younger.

His name was Niccolo San Tommaso — a name she'd heard before. *But when?* The employment file said he was a janitor at the museum. Odd — she'd been sure to expect a curator.

Yael scanned Falco's investigation reports that had been prepared by his lieutenant, Vespucci. And there she found it. Niccolo San Tommaso was the janitor who'd shared his coffee with the security guard on the night of the theft.

The record showed that San Tommaso had been hired in 1965. And in February 1974, just two months after the theft of the Magdalene Treasure, he'd taken leave to attend to his dying wife. Niccolo San Tommaso had never returned.

This was no coincidence. The dates closely bookended those of the thefts. All of the thefts. Including the gem-clad scepter — and the Aga Khan's manuscript.

Yael reexamined the employment file photo of Niccolo against the partial image of the thief pushing Bonnie. The two men were most certainly one and the same.

Age couldn't have been that illusory back in the Seventies. *Fuck no!* This meant that Niccolo the Elder, the janitor, didn't exist. He was a fictional character crafted in order to gain access to the Vatican.

Niccolo the Younger, the thief, was the real one. Master of disguise. Trickster extraordinaire.

Yael could guess what must have happened. Niccolo the Elder had drugged the Security Guard with the espresso, sending him to the toilet with his guts on fire. It obviously wasn't at all life-threatening yet still serious enough to ensure that Niccolo had enough time to enter Carlo's office unseen and remove the Globe and the Codex.

He could have hidden them in a cleaning cart or a rolling waste bin and concealed them in a supply room, where earlier he would have stashed a wheelchair from one of the many museum guard posts. He would have remained hidden overnight at the museum, waiting for the gates to open and his cohort to arrive.

The old janitor would never have been seen leaving the Vatican grounds because he'd have changed his appearance and become Niccolo the Younger! He'd fled from the Vatican with Bonnie — disguised as an anxious young couple rushing to deliver their baby.

CHAPTER 36

*Y*ael's mind was awhirl. The video has revealed that the *real* Carlo was Niccolo San Tommaso. If Vespucci's focus had not fallen so quickly to Carlo Rinaldi, he would have surely pieced this together.

Now Yael had new puzzles to sort. She flopped onto her back in the bed and stretched to her full length. Then she closed her eyes and watched clouds for a while.

When calm had returned, she focused her mind on the facts that mattered.

- Carlo Rinaldi had disappeared on the morning of the theft never to be seen again.
- Susan Bailey had also fallen off the radar in '73, just days before Carlo. And Susan's skillset in restoration made her the perfect candidate to be the crackerjack counterfeiter who'd forged more than thirty Papers over a half-dozen years.
- On the night of the gala, the surveillance video had caught Carlo entering the Vatican with a woman who no one had been able to identify.

- According to Falco, Carlo had entered the Vatican the morning of the theft through the employee entrance. And he hadn't been seen exiting that day, which is why he was presumed to be the man pushing the wheelchair.
- But now Tech's digital remastering made it clear that Carlo was *not* the wheelman who steered Bonnie and the Bronze Globe out of the gates. That role had been filled by Niccolo San Tommaso — a man who'd disguised himself as a janitor at the Vatican for years.

A short while ago Yael had been focused on the possibility of Chudnow as a third partner to Bonnie & Carlo — the man who'd have appeared under the bridge to ferry Bonnie & Carlo downriver, the man who she thought was last in possession of the Magdalene Treasure.

But now Yael had Niccolo. Unless Harry Chudnow *was* Niccolo San Tommaso.

In the cloud of unknowns, certain things were beginning to make sense. She had four suspects. Bonnie and Carlo and Susan and Niccolo — or Harry or whatever his real name was. Two had escaped unscathed while the other two had been killed in the accidental explosion.

Yael gasped. It was how she'd been thinking about the explosion that caught her breath. What if it hadn't been *accidental*?

What if the van's crash *wasn't* a reckless mistake? After all, every-thing else had been so well executed.

What if one of the pairs had rigged the explosion in order to double-cross their partners? If so, then they killed them and got away with the Magdalene Treasure as well as a fat chunk of change.

And now out of the blue almost fifty years later the thieving, murderous pair had surfaced again to send another ransom letter. It had to be them. Them or someone close to them.

But who was she looking for? Which two of the four?

Falco had told her that the burned corpses of a man and a woman had been found in the van. There was nothing in the files to back this up. Nothing had been recorded from the night of the failed final exchange, the night of the explosion or anytime thereafter because the investigation had been halted.

Falco was her only witness to the facts of the case. But how could she know for certain that he hadn't merely drawn a conclusion based on the events up to that point?

He'd been pursuing a man and a woman from the very beginning when Carlo had snuck someone into the museum on the night of the gala. And he'd seen them again on the day of the theft when video images captured the thieves as a pregnant young couple.

He'd also spotted them when Bonnie—or now possibly Susan—had ridden up on a motorcycle to take the ten million while Carlo or Niccolo had driven away in the van, revealing the lit fuse coiled around the wooden box.

But how could Yael know for certain *who exactly* had been in the van when it exploded? If it was a man and a woman, it could have been Bonnie and Niccolo or Susan and Carlo. There were actually four possibilities. And that's if the two in the van had in fact been a man and a woman.

There were still too many unknowns. It had been one thing to be chasing Carlo Rinaldi and an unknown Bonnie. But now she'd added Niccolo San Tommaso and Susan Bailey to the mix. There were too many *What-ifs* and too many possibilities. Any two one of the four could have survived. How would she know?

CHAPTER 37

*Y*ael went online to an archival news service and typed in the keywords that would target her search. It took only a moment before she was sifting through electronic pages, and a headline jumped out at her.

EXPLOSION ROCKS ROME.

Right around midnight on Christmas Eve 1973, a boy spied a man and a woman in the front of an old painter's van as it raced around a sharp corner near Aventine Hill before barreling past him and down the steep road. The boy was thrown to the ground when the van suddenly exploded in a firebomb.

He'd been the first to call the police. Unfortunately, the boy had given no description of the man or the woman. It had all happened too fast.

The article went on to say that the cause of the explosion was unknown. Both the driver and the passenger had been killed in the fire. Military police had refused to comment. But their presence led the writer to speculate that mafia was involved, possibly an escalation to the long-standing feud between Italian crime families.

Yael scoured through more newspapers and found additional articles on the accident. But none of them had anything new to add. What she did notice was that each of the local papers had also reported on a second curious event that occurred in Rome on Christmas Eve, 1973.

It was the headline in *Il Messaggero* that captured it best. In English it would have read, *MEDICAL SCHOOL TOMFOOLERY, BODIES TAKEN.* Two cadavers had been reported missing and presumed stolen from the training department of the Sapienza University Hospital in Rome. Police questioned the college fraternities. Mischief was suspected.

Yael dropped the tablet to her lap. According to the paper, both the van explosion and the theft of the cadavers had happened the day *before* the newspaper's publication — on December 25. But Falco hadn't absconded with the burnt corpses to dispose of them until the day *after* the explosion, on December 26.

What was this?

She knew the answer before her mind stopped spinning. The bodies in the van were the stolen cadavers from the med school, the same corpses that Francesco had later fed to the sharks. They'd been cleverly cast in the role of the thieves.

Everything had been staged!

There had been no misstep to cause the accident. No oafishness at all. The entire escapade had been planned to perfection in order that the thieves could escape intact with the Magdalene Treasure.

The explosion of the van had been their final coup. The melted bronze had been staged. The metal box had been staged. Even the clasps of the knapsack supposedly-containing the ten million dollars had been staged. And so had the corpses.

The explosion wasn't a reckless accident at all. It was a brilliantly calculated subterfuge rigged to go off exactly how it did. Exactly where it did. Exactly when it did.

The final exchange had been a charade. The thieves had planned it from the very beginning. First to make four look like two and then to stage their deaths and the loss of both objects so the investigation would come to an end. They'd planned it in order to get away with the precious relics intact, to get away without forever being chased.

Their plan was beyond brilliant, and Yael was astonished at how well it had been executed.

The investigation had been closed. The thieves had triumphed. They had gotten away with the Globe, the Codex and ten million dollars — and God only knew how much else from their earlier thefts.

CHAPTER 38

*W*ith a newfound excitement, Yael returned her attention to what was bearing fruit. The videos.

She scanned backward and forward taking in every detail. This time she noticed an interesting anomaly. Video had captured the image of a boy running into the Vatican fifteen minutes after the gates had opened.

It just didn't fit. Why run? And why alone?

Yael dialed quickly. Tech picked up on the first ring.

"Are you still synched with me on the video?"

"Yes."

"Zoom in on the boy," she said. "He looks what—? Fifteen?"

"Younger," said Tech.

"What's he wearing? The shoes. Show me the shoes!"

"Hightops, I think," said Tech, honing in on the shot. "Yes, Converse hightops."

"Hold this image and show me the woman in the wheelchair again."

Tech pulled up the image.

"Go forward slowly," Yael said, her words rushing out in a blur. "There! Stop! Focus in on the shoes. Can you do that?"

The pregnant woman's skirt was hiked up to mid-calf in the shot, buoyed by the hidden Globe on her lap. Visible beneath the hemline was the same pair of natty, vintage hightop sneakers worn by the boy.

Yael's mind was afire as she tried to fit this new piece into her puzzle. The accomplice of Carlo and Niccolo, this elusive pregnant mystery woman, was really a child!

The thieves had intended to conjure the pretense of a daring couple. And they'd been careful throughout to avoid revealing the boy. From the pregnant woman on the surveillance video to the woman on the motorcycle at the blue-basket exchange. Both had been the boy.

Even the woman who'd entered the Vatican with Carlo the night of the Sistine Chapel Gala.

Yael's mind was flying now as she set the few remaining pieces in place. Only one other boy had ever appeared in the investigation — the one from the newspaper article who'd witnessed the explosion.

Yael closed her eyes to reimagine the events. If the van explosion had been staged, then there was no way the cadavers could have steered the van around a corner and down a hill before bursting into flames the way that the boy had reported to the police. The vehicle must have been stopped at the top of the hill while the cadavers were set into place, then left to roll down the hill and explode.

The boy had described something very different. Because he hadn't *witnessed* it. *He'd been a part of it!*

"Give me the boy again! A frame of him running into the Vatican!"

Tech brought up the frozen image.

"Show me the face!"

The boy's head filled up the screen. The eyes and brow matched those of the pregnant woman.

It took another moment for the rest of his features to sink in. Yael sat and stared as it all became clear. She was dumbfounded by who she saw.

It wasn't necessary for Tech to perform a digital age-progression for Yael's surety to set in. She'd just needed to open her eyes to the possibility of yet another great orchestration and an equally outstanding performance. Though this time, rather than Falco or Vespucci or Adolfos Sideris being duped, *Yael* was the fool.

The very thought wrought thundering waves of outrage. Yael's sea was aboil.

CHAPTER 39

*Y*ael spied grey clouds barreling in from the west as her helicopter touched down in a sleepy central park. It was still early morning, and the rain was inbound. In no time at all, there would be a deluge.

Pigeons took flight at the sight of the bigger bird, leaving their marks on an otherwise beautiful statue of Apollo. Why had the great ancient god not carried sun to this day?

A small dog stood at the end of his taut tether and barked unceasingly. His master stared dumbly while Yael leapt from the chopper and raced through the grassy field. Across the road in the circular drive of a swanky hotel, an old Mercedes sat with an open trunk. A valet was lifting the last of the luggage out of the rear.

Yael sprinted to the car and jumped in. Ignoring the shouts from behind, she slid the keys off the dash and brought it to life with one simple turn. She spun onto the road, sending rubber and smoke to her tail.

Within her grasp were the Bronze Globe and the Magdalene Prophecy.

And vengeance!

~

*A*pproaching from the road, Yael could see her mark leaned over the open hood of his classic DB5. He made an adjustment that brought the idle right to its sweet spot. He toyed with the throttle cable, revving the Aston's engine. The rumble was that of a dozen lions roaring in concert.

The wind had picked up and drizzle was spotting the silver paint with spectral dots. The sleek snout of the sports car was pointed at her, shielding the man's face with the rear-angled hood.

And then he stood, his eyes still fixed to the car.

It was like she was seeing him for the first time. A perfect match for the age-progressed computer image Tech had ultimately given her. Although with one glaring difference — he looked younger than his fifty-seven years. She was overcome by his appearance, just as she had been when she'd lain by his side only a short while before.

Thomas.

Thomas who'd loved her. Thomas who'd betrayed her.

Thomas who'd now know her fury.

Yael neared, the crunch of the gravel beneath her feet obscured by the thundering motor. His nose was buried again, deep in the engine.

"Hey!" she shouted over the twelve burbling cylinders.

He lifted his head, startled.

"Oh! Yael, what a surprise!" He moved to embrace her, but the ice in her eyes held him off.

"I wish… I wish I could… God! You— You lied to me!" Yael's voice rose to a scream. "HOW COULD YOU?!"

He shook his head in confusion. "I'm sorry Yael. I'm not sure what—"

"Goddamnit, Thomas! You fucked with the wrong woman! You still don't know. It was your *statue*. It led me here," she said pointing to the distant grove of trees.

He took a casual step back, distancing himself from her.

"But then your performance. What a show of affection!" her voice peaked in anger. "YOU DUPED ME! MADE ME A FOOL!"

Thomas took another step backward, but this time she followed.

"Now you wonder why I'm here? You really have no clue?"

She shook her head in disgust, savoring the blow that came next. "Your hightops gave you away!"

Lines appeared on Thomas's forehead as his eyes swung into space, forced to replay a far distant memory.

"You might have made a convincing woman once upon a time, but now you've been found."

A cocoon of silence fell over him. Yael could see that his senses were shocked. His worst fears had come alive.

"The Bronze Globe. The Codex. Where are they?" she demanded. Her words were staccato. Clear and precise.

Thomas locked eyes with hers as she inched closer. A bead of sweat rolled down his nose and hovered near the tip.

All of a sudden a blinding flash dazzled Yael. It was coupled with an immediate and incredibly loud boom of thunder that blasted her very heart.

The lightning smacked a tree towering over them with a frightening crack. They both looked up as a heavy branch came barreling down. Thomas leapt out of the way while Yael rolled clear. Seconds later they stood face to face, yards from the fallen debris.

Before she could act, Thomas suddenly dropped and thrust his legs out toward her. He clipped her knee sharply with his heel. A second hard kick to her torso and she crumpled to the ground, reeling in pain and breathless, the wind knocked clear of her lungs.

Thomas dove into his idling beast and spun the wheels. The fine gravel pummeled Yael like a spray of stone bullets. When grip finally came, the car fishtailed a moment, then propelled forward with a staggering thrust.

He sped away, the distance quickly growing between them.

CHAPTER 40

*Y*ael screamed. It was a scream of anger not hurt. She would not scream for pain. Not on this day. To have come this close and be outmaneuvered— It made her blood boil. She had underestimated him. Yet again!

The ill-timed twin strike of lightning and thunder had spooked her. It must have been right above them.

The Quickening! Could it have been?

It was just in that fraction of a second that Thomas had bested her. And then hailstones from hell had erupted to punish her misstep.

In India, in pursuit of the dream of the Perfect Warrior, Yael had once run up a steep mountainside with raw rice strewn inside her socks. She'd survived this feat of forbearance by sheer will alone, mind over matter, steadying her thoughts on the finish line ten miles away rather than the butchery taking place on the soles of her feet.

She would do so again.

Yael took stock of herself. The front of her body had taken the full force of the stoning. Pockmarks covered her where the pebbles had made batter of flesh. Her forehead, cheeks, chin, and lips stung. Her left eye hurt badly. The thin veil of clothing she'd worn had lent little protection from the projectiles.

She could taste the rusty-salt mix of her blood and her sweat and the now-pelting rain as they rolled past her lips.

Yael had been on the ground when Thomas fled in the Aston. Now with her breath recovered, she lifted herself upright. Her knee screamed out from where his kick had landed, throwing echoes of pain up and down her body. But thankfully, it didn't feel broken.

Yael hobbled to where she'd left the Mercedes just out of sight. Pain joined her every step until finally she reached the car and threw herself into the hard leather seat.

She quickly brought it to life, slammed her foot to the floor and raced the car in reverse onto the road, masterfully cranking the wheel while shifting into first. The car spun around with its own momentum. Without touching the brakes, she popped the clutch and gassed the car forward. It gripped the wet tarmac and accelerated hard. Yael followed where Thomas had gone, toward the south of the island.

She climbed the main road to the top of a rise and screeched to a stop. Below her ahead was the center of town, where ferries and boats and escape would be found.

But Yael now knew the mind she was chasing. Rather than go into town, where people and cars would counter his flight, Thomas would head somewhere else.

She craned her neck to take in the large number of boats moored all over the coast. Any one of those marinas could be his way out. He would have stayed to the east to skirt as much of the traffic as possible.

And then she saw it. Off in the distance, a sleek, silver car zipped through the rain and across the bridge to the adjacent isle.

She had him!

CHAPTER 41

*T*homas had raced through the eastern fringes of Maddalena before crossing to Isola Caprera. Yael would not think to follow him to the nature preserve where there were little else but old forest pines.

He drove into the heart of the island and pulled to a stop some ten yards down a small dirt lane. The state park couldn't provide his escape but would buy him some time to plot his next move.

He eased his grip on the wheel, relaxed his head back in the seat and stared blankly as the wipers cleared his view.

After all these years! *How on earth?* Snared by the statue and his old Converse sneakers! Could the clues have been more obscure?

In a world of a billion haystacks, Yael had dared to thread a single lost needle. It was unfathomable!

The Treasure was safe for the moment. Maybe not so for long.

Thomas pulled out his mobile and dialed.

*Y*ael flew toward the bridge to Caprera.

She pushed the coupe at lightning speed, no thought to anyone or thing in her way. Her senses were heightened, near breaking.

The rain which started at Thomas's place had turned now into a deluge that fell in sheets. Just one unseen puddle, one misplaced turn of the wheel, and the car would spin out of control.

At this speed, death would be a welcome end.

~

*A*s Thomas sat with his phone to his ear, a pale yellow blur flashed in the mirror followed immediately by the screeching of tires on the slippery road behind him.

Yael!

He dropped the phone in his lap and sent the car barreling backward to the road. As it jumped onto the tarmac, his Aston slammed hard into the front of Yael's Mercedes, which by then she'd managed to turn around.

He craned his head to see through the steam spouting from its hood. Yael was fuming.

He threw his car into first, but the two bumpers were desperately coupled. He spun his wheels hard. The car rocked from left to right before suddenly breaking free with a metallic crack.

He raced away back over the bridge. The Aston's steel bumper dragged clamorously on the soaked roadway until it finally fell away.

~

*I*t took Yael a dozen thundering heartbeats to restart her engine. When finally it fired, she followed Thomas as he sped back to Maddalena.

Her car was grinding. Steam blew from the hood. Blood still

dripped from her brow. With her foot pressed firmly to the limit, she pushed the car to gain all manner of speed.

Faster and faster she went over the bridge to the north of the island. She gave no thought to the twists and the turns in the road, even less to the puddles and pools.

She drove blindly, straight into the quickening storm.

CHAPTER 42

*T*homas flew onto the coastal ring road carved into the rock. To one side was a sheer granite face, to the other a cliffside drop to the punishing sea.

He could see the busted Mercedes trailing in the distance, still racing the curves. It sputtered and blew steam like an angry locomotive.

The wind tossed the rain in gusts. The gray skies became grayer. The sun was fallen prey to a stormy eclipse.

Thomas white-knuckled the wheel as he urged his car faster. The road was like a ribbon unfurling in the wind. Speed was his only escape.

He could feel Yael bearing down from behind, and his belly clenched.

It happened suddenly. The road pulled sharply to the right. The back tires lost grip for only a second and fishtailed around the bend.

Up ahead, a man stood directly in his path — someone caught in the storm, hoping for a ride, rain-soaked and frightened and looking straight at Thomas with what could only be terror in his eyes. For a moment nothing existed but the two men facing each other in a thunderous flash of forever.

Then the sun ripped through the darkness, blinding Thomas. For an instant, the road disappeared. Everything slowed. The world suspended mid-spin as if he'd touched the very core of a tornado.

His heartbeat threw but one mighty thump. Thomas felt suddenly animated and enlivened as if he'd just donned a cloak woven from the skin of electric eels.

What followed was a jumble of images and sounds as the Aston Martin bounced between cliff wall and guardrail, guardrail and cliff wall, smashing and spinning and tumbling its way to one last cacophonous crash.

CHAPTER 43

hen Thomas stirred, a veil was descending over his crown and his eyes. He shook it loose as best he could, but the crash had left him feeling dazed and displaced.

Thomas wobbled away from the wreckage. On the ground before him was the horribly mangled hitchhiker, just barely alive. Lying on his back. Legs splayed cruelly. Left-arm bent and broken. Bone protruding skin.

The man's chest had been crushed. Blood oozed from his head, coating everything in red. Life was draining slowly away. A powerful surge shot through Thomas like a wild current. There was not a thing he could do.

As if underwater, his senses altered by shock, Thomas heard the muffled roar of Yael's car drawing near. His thoughts jumped to the Most Treasured of Treasures. Yael had come close to the Bronze Globe several times by now, yet still, it was hidden. But it wouldn't be long before she'd unravel the clues. And then what?

Thomas dashed to the road's edge and sprang up and over the rail, giving no thought to what lay beyond, a frightened deer escaping its prey. He landed hard on a little rock outcrop sharply sloped to the sea and tried desperately to grasp for a hold. He struggled until he could no more.

Finally, his fingers ceded their purchase, and he slipped and tumbled to one last boulder beneath. It was now the only thing that spared him the hundred-foot dash to the jagged shore below.

He lay on his back and stared up at his granite awning. The ledge angled steeply some ten feet above like the half-open lid of a giant sarcophagus.

Suddenly, a great burst of light flashed with the most rippingest crack of thunder. Hope and fear in one awesome play.

Then nothing.

A cascade of emotions welled up like a nest of spiders coming to life in his body, biting and stinging and spitting their toxin. Fear eclipsed all.

Here he lay alone and broken, like prey bound in some trapper's snare. When would his huntress come?

～

*I*t was much darker now than before, a darkness greater than that wrought by tempest alone.

Suddenly, from the menacing silence came a dull buzzing, like a dozen bees encircling his ears, the hum of their flaps disarming, confusing and lulling. Had his mind made trickery to soothe the sting of his fate?

Thomas seemed to have lost all sobriety, a drunken fool alone in his wasteland. Nothing seemed real.

It was as if he hung in the final moments of exhaustion on the precipice of sleep.

～

*T*homas skidded to a stop in front of an open market. He revved the twelve-cylinder engine hard before turning it off then rose from the car with a bounce and beelined the fruit stand.

He picked up the brightest of blood oranges and drew in its bouquet.

The old Gypsy vendor in her flowery dress reached across and took hold of his wrist.

"You drive very fast," she glared.

His grin stayed hidden behind the succulent Tarocco.

Her hold stayed firm, along with her stare.

"I see you in my dreams!" she cried in a strained whisper. "You drive very, very fast. Near La Piramide."

What was she talking about?

"Il faro," she said simply, pointing off in the distance.

What lighthouse?

"Do not fear. I see he will come for you."

Thomas nodded politely, handed her some coins, pocketed the fruit and climbed the grassy hill above the plaza. He followed a path that climbed higher and higher until he reached the plateau.

The horizon revealed the ageless blue of the Mediterranean. It sparkled through the curling waves as if a million fireworks had erupted, then a million more.

Ahead in the skyline, a hawk caught his eye as it flew toward him. Straight forward it came, closer and closer, growing larger and larger. Thomas could feel his heart racing.

And in the very last moment, the hawk changed into a brilliant ball of light and flew right through him.

~

*T*homas awoke with a start to a dazzling flash. He tensed for the rumble of thunder to follow. Oddly, it didn't.

Another bright flash lit up the sky, again without boom. In the span of its twilight, Thomas glimpsed a shadow off in the distance. A strangely shaped structure.

The sky seemed suddenly bright. But wherefrom this brightness? There could be no sun at this hour of night.

Something had changed. The distant flash of light was now

unmoving. It shined fully upon him. Beneath the light, a pyramid appeared — an old rocky lighthouse.

La Piramide!

Out of its shadow, another image appeared. It grew larger with each passing moment. The hawk! It flew down from the lighthouse and right toward Thomas.

Again his heartbeat quickened, when suddenly, beneath the glare of the lighthouse, the hawk just disappeared.

In its place was a man — a very tall man dressed in loose linen. He moved lithely over the cliffside rocks as if it was sport.

When finally he appeared, the tall man knelt next to Thomas. Not one word was spoken.

Drained of all strength, Thomas rolled his eyes back up to the sky. And darkness came.

~

The tall man carried Thomas like a sleeping child slowly up the stone steps. La Piramide sat perched high atop a rocky tor.

The huge wooden door creaked open loudly.

"What is this place?" Thomas said weakly. His face was quite pale now.

"The lighthouse," the man replied.

As he carried Thomas across the threshold, a gust of wind mixed with rain, leaves, twigs, and dirt chased them inside.

A beautiful woman with silken grey hair arose from the hearth, where a bold fire crackled its welcome. The couple set Thomas down on a thick bearskin rug.

"I was in the lantern room when I saw you stranded on the rocks," said the woman. "You lost your ship in the storm."

"No, not a ship…," Thomas said, but exhaustion left his thought unfinished.

"We saw that you could not climb to us for safe haven," the man said. "So I came down to you."

"I was told of this place."

"Yes? You will be safe here."

"Who are you?"

"I am Ariella," said the woman. "This is our lighthouse. We are the caretakers."

～

CHAPTER 44

$\mathscr{T}$homas stirred in terror at the sound of a shutter banging. The wind howled and buffeted the walls. Rain outside fell in torrents.

He looked about frantically trying to make sense of this place he now found himself in. The walls were an intricate lattice of teak, bearing imagery much like the occult symbols in an Egyptian tomb.

In toto, he felt like he could have been looking at an ornate wooden tapestry. Whose story did it tell?

In the very center of the room was a large open column running right to the top. It was a staircase with the feel of an Escher, a spiral labyrinth leading mysteriously to higher chambers.

The tall man appeared and drew close. "You are safe," he said.

"What happened to me?"

"Do you not remember?"

Thomas searched in his thoughts. "I was driving. I crashed. But why am I here?"

Thomas tried to lift himself from the floor, but the caretaker placed a gentle hand on his shoulder. "You cannot leave this place in your state. The storm is too great. We must wait for it to ease."

"No," said Thomas, shaking his head.

And with great effort, he rose from the rug and made his way to the large wooden door. He tried to pull it open, but the wind howled and sucked in protest. The door held as if thickly glued to the jamb.

"Help me! Please," he begged of the caretaker.

The tall man moved to lend his strength to the effort, pulling the door with both hands. It budged only briefly and then slammed shut again.

"I have been through this many times," he explained. "It is because of where we are. The wind is too wild. It must be brought to calm before you can move on safely from here. We will get through this. Soon it will pass."

Thomas collapsed into the tall man's strong arms and began to fade.

"It is not so good for you to sleep," the caretaker said.

"I'm tired," said Thomas. "And I'm cold."

The man draped a rough blanket over Thomas. He then stoked the fire and added a log.

"Come, let us talk. I am Gabo. What shall I call you, dear boy?"

Boy? Thomas had only to raise his eyebrows.

"Ah, if only you knew how many days I have seen," said Gabo. "It would not be so strange to you."

"I'm Thomas."

The fire now roared in the hearth throwing flickering shadows all about. It frightened him. as if it was trying to show Thomas something he wasn't seeing.

"I have told you I will keep you safe from the storm. But know this, my boy, you are safe here from *anything* that threatens you."

Tears and redness filled Thomas's eyes as he choked back his grief.

"There was a man on the road. I think I..." he said, halting. "I hit him with my car. And I left him alone." Thomas sobbed weakly. "He was... Blood everywhere. His head. His chest. He was dying."

～

CHAPTER 45

*T*he clip-clop of bone-heeled shoes on stone roused Thomas again. Ariella emerged from the Escher carrying a brass tray bearing trinkets. She walked with a palpable peace, an ease filled with grace and dignity. She wore a light, ankle-length tunic. A simple silk scarf covered her head. She was remarkably beautiful. Ageless in appearance yet clearly old in her mien.

With a long set of tongs, she reached into the hearth and plucked a round, flat stone slightly larger than the size of her palm. It glowed red as she placed it in a perfectly shaped open locket on her ceremonial tray.

Thomas watched as she snapped the locket shut and slid it into a beautifully embroidered pouch. Her movements were effortless and fluid like she'd practiced them a thousand times before.

Ariella held the pouch in both hands like she was praying and with eyes closed raised it to her forehead, to her lips and last to her heart. Then she opened her eyes and placed the covered stone on Thomas's belly.

She smiled at Thomas kindly but said nothing. Her hands hung a few inches above his stomach. After a moment she lowered them, left upon right atop the stone, and pressed ever so slightly. The fire immediately moved to the core of his gut, as if he'd swallowed a lump of hot coal.

He wanted to clench his muscles, but the heat was slackening them. It was an odd sensation, a struggle between grasping and letting go. The latter was winning.

Thomas shivered despite the heat in his belly, the thick blanket that covered him and the crackling fire. His eyes penetrated Ariella's searchingly, making plain his exhaustion. He tried to form words, but none could be heard.

Ariella scanned him, feeling as much as seeing. She seemed to be taking in the full extent of his injuries. Thomas's bruises were deep. So too his cuts. She then raised her hands over him, holding them still.

He quickly felt waves of heat moving into his body. When her hands settled over Thomas's lower torso, he began to twitch and then to shake.

Ariella didn't bat a lid, nor did she move her hands. She stayed as she was and began to sing like a Gaelic songstress. She leaned in and hummed right into his ears.

The effect was immediately calming. Magically soothing. The palsy ebbed and a greater sense of peace fell upon him.

Thomas found the strength to whisper, "Thank you. How—?"

"We have many gifts, dear one," Ariella said, her eyes filled with kindness.

Thomas's eyes began to wander.

"Do not sleep, my boy. Your condition is delicate," she said, gently caressing his head as if she knew that her touch held him from slipping. "Won't you tell me about your life? When you were just a boy?"

She hummed ever so softly, a melody Thomas hadn't heard in a long time.

He was just a boy, four years old, and could hear his mother singing while she cooked. He stood in the hallway outside the kitchen, just out of her sight.

She was different with the hymns. Calmer. Less angry. It was the only time he ever got close to feeling her love. Even though it wasn't a love for him, only her love for a distant God far up in the clouds.

On Sundays, they'd gather in church to hear of salvation. Their brimstone Baptist preacher would say more to frighten his flock than to make way for peace. Thomas would look up at the crucified Jesus and wonder if this was really what he'd had in his mind.

Thomas had long since come to understand that his parents hadn't seen the hellfire they'd brought into their home. They hadn't grasped the emptiness that came from such abject devotion to a critical God.

Nor had they been able to see the angst in Thomas that had grown from it all.

CHAPTER 46

Thomas's mother and father were strict and stiffer than boards. He dared not speak unless spoken to first. He wasn't even sure his parents had ever held his hand, except to pull him to the garage so he'd be out of the way whenever the minister came by for the weekly neighborhood revivals.

It was on these evenings that Thomas would escape into another world as he played with all of his father's locksmithing tools.

At night, he would lie awake and wonder why God had placed him there. What had he ever done so to deserve such a miserable life?

Thomas always had the feeling he'd just done something terribly wrong without knowing quite what.

'Why do you punish me?' his mother would yell.

Thomas was either too late or too noisy or too nothing at all. After a while, it struck him that it was simply that he was too visible. If he could change that, maybe he could survive.

Locks had become an invitation for Thomas, not a deterrent. One day he'd snuck into the hardware store and plucked some fancy crates and a small sheet of plywood. He built himself a simple desk in the cellar of his home, in the dankest, darkest corner where no one dared come. His chair had been rolled from the same store's back office.

In time, Thomas discovered that his refuge was really his doorway to freedom. He'd climb onto his desk and shimmy through a small casement window set high in the wall. He never once let himself be caught nor ever left it open for fear of attracting more wrath — and the loss of his only sliver of relief, his portal to invisibility.

Studying for school was impossible at home. There was always too much tension to focus his mind. But he listened well in class, and that often proved enough. Whenever it didn't, he'd wait for his parents to fall sleep then escape through his portal to study in the school library.

One day, even that wasn't enough, and Thomas found himself wandering the school halls to his classroom, picking door locks and desk locks and any other lock that came in his way. There he discovered he could simply study with the next day's exam papers.

It was late in his elementary school years that Thomas was introduced to archery. It was a solitary sport that he took to with ease. An hour a day just wasn't enough, and so Thomas took it upon himself to continue his practice with the best of the bows he'd taken one night from the equipment cage in the gymnasium. Another invitation he just couldn't refuse.

Thomas's invisibility now spread into the day. He'd go down the steps to the cellar and then quickly climb out the window, towing his bow and arrows behind him.

When simple target practice lost its challenge, Thomas let himself into the town's flower shop and lifted a small tank of helium and a big box of balloons. He was up at dawn the next morning floating balloons high in the sky and testing his skill.

Thomas hadn't even realized how much time he'd spent honing his skill. Had he thought about it, he might have noticed when it first started to feel like the bow was an extension to his arm. In the same way that he didn't have to think when he raised a fingernail to an itch, so too Thomas had merely to spy his target and the arrow was cast, each time reaching its mark perfectly.

～

CHAPTER 47

One year later, when the gym teacher brought out the archery equipment again for the children, Thomas bedazzled her with his skill. Each shot hit the bullseye.

After school, she set up the targets at increasing distances. Again, every one of Thomas's arrows found the red dot.

One day, she informed him that the coach of the American National Archery Team wanted to see him. The coach set up two adjacent targets and instructed Thomas to follow his lead.

This time, not one of his arrows hit the mark. Instead, he landed one arrow after another right atop the dumbfounded coach's arrows on the adjacent target.

Thomas's mother and father were oblivious to his accomplishments in archery — or his accomplishments in anything, for that matter. It had taken the vociferous insistence of the gym teacher, the principal as well as the national coach to convince them to let Thomas tour with the National team that year. In the end, it was probably the thought of a child-free home that swayed them most. He was just ten years old.

For Thomas, stepping out in the world was more exciting than he knew life could be. He won competition after competition, besting the best from the U.S., Europe and beyond.

All of this happened in one whirlwind year and culminated in him earning an invitation to travel to Munich with the 1972 U.S. Olympic Team. He was too young to compete, but the team coach wanted him to experience the Olympics to prepare for the next one in four years when he *would* fit the age bracket.

In Munich, Thomas shined during practice, dazzling all who watched his fluid display of art. When the day of the finals came, Thomas's coach wanted him front and center in the arena.

"Next time, it'll be you out there," he said, pointing to the competing athletes. "Nothing can prepare you for the feelings — excitement and worry, anticipation and fear. The winner is not always the better athlete but rather the one who is better able to deal with his nerves. You can win the gold in four years. And it'll change your world."

Thomas escaped to the washroom for a moment alone before the final round began. He stood in front of the mirror reflecting on how good he felt. It was the attention he was getting, the joy of being recognized for doing something well. And it was the *freedom* to be his best, the *freedom* to shine.

In four years he could win the gold. In four years his world could change.

And at that moment as *four years* rang in his ears, he made a bold choice. Thomas walked from the bathroom and turned left out the door. Away from his coach. Away from his teammates. Away from the cheers and the crowds. And toward the one thing he'd come to treasure most above all.

Freedom.

CHAPTER 48

*L*eucadia, California was now eight hours in the rearview mirror. Isabelle Merchant had spent most of the long drive through the desert singing along to a looping set of tracks she'd once made for Marie to get them in the mood for Arizona. They were love songs by the likes of Linda Ronstadt, Stevie Nicks and Lynda Carter, the original Wonder Woman. Her favorite was a Billy Joel classic, *The Ballad of Billy the Kid*. The words rolled off Isa's tongue like she'd learned them just yesterday.

When she carved through the Arizona mountains, across the final pass and at last into Sedona, a swell of emotion flooded through her. *Marie had loved this incredible oasis!*

And though Isa was alone, there was a comfort to be found in the spectacular red rocks that towered into the sky. The formations were believed to be sacred in their energetic resonance with higher dimensional frequencies.

Sedona was a spiritual hub. Psychics and healers displayed their offerings on sidewalk sign-boards much like the all-you-can-eat buffets did in the back streets of Vegas. While some of it was flighty and unreliable, there was at the same time a strong undercurrent of integrity in a still small but growing number of mystical practitioners.

In the end, it was the palpable energy of the rocks and their inherent beauty that had always appealed so much to both Marie and Isa.

It was as Isa wound her way to the beautiful hotel her mother had favored that she lost track of how fast she was driving. Suddenly she'd gone from rural highway to Sedona's main thoroughfare and found herself racing toward some cars idling at a red light.

She had no time to stop and swung the car to the opening on the left. As she barreled into the intersection, she whipped onto the cross street and just missed getting T-boned by a huge pickup.

Her heart was now pounding. Excitement. Not fear. And rather than retrace her path, Isa crossed deeper into the back hills northwest of town.

She followed the pavement till she veered to another. This one was very quiet with almost no one in sight. It curved gently left and right and in places steeply up and down.

It was on one particular down sweep that out of the corner of her eye Isabelle caught a flourish of color.

She wasn't sure what she'd seen, but the scent of flowers filled her senses. Lots of flowers.

And in that very moment, the dam to her tears broke. She remembered her mother's words to her. *Look for me in the flowers.*

In the home they had lived for as long as Isabelle could remember, one of her mother's purest joys was her rose bushes. They were everywhere. In front of the house. In back of the house. Yellow roses, pink roses, and white roses.

But none was so precious to Marie as red roses. 'They are the color of love,' she'd say. 'Smell them. You'll see I am right.' And she'd always been right.

One of the last things that she had managed to speak to Isabelle—while her life was slowly fading from her voice and her sight—was, 'Look for me in the flowers. Look and you will always remember how much I love you.'

Isabelle quickly spun her convertible around and parked in front of what appeared to be a spectacular villa. The flourish of color she'd seen turned out to be *hundreds* of flowers. Everywhere.

Isabelle couldn't resist the attraction and walked onto the grounds. A very soft-spoken and gracious host gave her a royal tour of the property. It was built into an arc of steep hills. Pools had been set against waterfalls and granite boulders. Everywhere she stood, Isa found herself gifted with unending views of the spectacular red rock horizon.

The focal point of the resort was the most incredible spa. It hung dramatically over a cliff and peppered one of the slopes with satin-walled teepees for massage, a trio of plunge pools, a magical hobbit-house sauna and a hilltop gazebo for the practice of yoga.

In the heart of the property was a small cave. A tight twist of sage burned within, perhaps an homage to the Hopi tribe who'd once called this land their home. Isabelle closed her eyes for a spell. The peace was palpable. It was like a penetrating aura of loving somnolence.

Elsewhere on the property in the very center of a meditation pond, a lotus flower floated silently. As her gaze softened, the lotus became a rose. Its white beauty turned red, and Isabelle felt her mother's love enwrap her like a shawl of fragrant petals.

'Love never dies, my sweet,' she heard her mother's voice say.

Isa gasped.

And then again. Her mother's voice. As soft as a whisper in the wind.

'Now seek the Most Treasured of Treasures.'

CHAPTER 49

*E*xhaustion overcame her that afternoon. Isa lay on the bed in her suite and dreamt.

It was a dream and yet not a dream. Richer than a dream. Somehow deeper than a dream and yet more real than any dream she'd ever dreamt — for on some level she felt fully awake.

She dreamed of the little girl from the bedtime stories her mother had read when Isa was just a child — when Isa had been so completely mesmerized by the wondrous tales of the Patagonian girl Meigga and her pet jaguar Yaga.

It wasn't the first time Isa had dreamt of the girl. But it was the first time in at least twenty years. And somehow this time Isa *was* Meigga, not just dreaming of her.

Meigga was draped in silks so fine they were transparent, so light that they could scarcely be felt. She was standing atop a spiral cobbled-stone stairway. It felt smooth to her bare feet.

To her left, the walls were earthen, solid and cool to the touch. To her right was the inside of the coil, where the open depths below were hidden by darkness.

Yaga had retreated into the darkness, his golden eyes slowly dimming to black.

Meigga spun her way down and down and down the steps, gently to the unknown below. A delicate light emanated from her dress. It was enough to show what was immediately before her, nothing more. She felt solemn and sublime as if she'd arisen from a deep meditation. It was this reverence alone that carried her forward and downward step after step.

If clouds could be made to embody the boundless love of a mother, then it would best be described that Meigga was descending into a most beautiful, soft cloud — more sublime with every turn of her spiral step.

Breathing was effortless, and she noticed she had come into a rhythm that drew in the cloud-mist through her breath—deep, deep into her being—and then released it back into her surroundings. Again and again.

She felt all sensations simultaneously. Meigga's luminescent gown. The smooth steps. The cool wall. And the great, indescribable reverence. Even though she was becoming ever more light-headed the further she descended, her clarity did not suffer. She remained acutely aware of everything she was experiencing.

The final steps were much broader and slowed her pace. When at last they leveled to the floor, Meigga halted and found herself looking in the distance at a large wooden box. It was oddly lit from far above, from the place she had come, the light somehow ceding all but the crate into darkness.

It appeared as if the solitary object sat upon a magnificent altar raised to the Gods. Or was it resting on a column that rose out of the depths, a stone obelisk from the netherworld?

The box was the center of her attention. The center of all attention. Nothing else existed. If not for the subtle glow emanating from her dress, she wouldn't even have had a sense of herself in that space.

There was something other-worldly about the box. It was beckoning her. Or was it taunting her? She couldn't decide.

She'd been motionless since reaching the bottom of the stairs and now noticed a fear rising within her. The space before her felt like a chasm, the darkness a void as if she might drop into oblivion if she dared to cross.

Yet still, the box called.

CHAPTER 50

*M*eigga probed her feelings, but excitement and anticipation swung freely on the same fulcrum as fear. The darkness seemed darker now. Somehow her dress shed less light.

And then a thought. Had she been holding her breath all this time? Meigga inhaled deeply, drawing in the full breadth of air that her chest would allow.

She immediately felt herself lighten, a feeling of love swept through her. The mother cloud had returned. And with it came a lightening of her dress, even more than before.

Meigga saw the floor appear in the space between where she now stood and the wooden box. Without further thought, she moved across the span and knelt before the altar. She found herself atop the finest of sand that cosseted her knees.

Meigga was now enveloped by the same light from above, a luminescent cocoon enshrouding her with the box. Now she could see that it wasn't a box but rather an old and oddly-shaped chest with intricate carvings.

She passed her hands over its wooden surface, feeling the grooves of each ancient etching like they were the scars of her life.

A huge swell of heavy emotion rose from within her, much more powerful than before. She felt overcome and her thoughts were scrambled. It felt as if she were atop a massive geyser being blasted by forces from a well deep, deep within.

It took all she had to hold herself together as all manner of darkness rocked her being.

Fear. Anger. Grief. Despair.

Meigga was in a state of complete abandon, in total submission to the power of these forces as they swept through her. And yet this was not quite as it was, for the emotions were not from *outside* her. They erupted from within to issue forth all manner of ugliness.

And then somewhere in the recesses of her consciousness, it was *Isa* who remembered her mother reading to her each night as a child. She recalled the words that had seemed too hard to comprehend, the words that now moved her to tears,

---

Beloved Girl, remember the paradox. You must accept not only the good in your life but also everything within you that has not been good. Only then can you know your true magnificence.

As Isa let the newly charged understanding of those words permeate Meigga, the flood of emotions subsided and she felt lightened anew.

Gone was the fog of confusion. She now understood that the love Meigga had been imbibing from her mother-cloud was a brilliant reflection of her very own love — a love of *acceptance*.

This love now poured from Meigga's as the carvings on the ancient chest revealed themselves with the clarity of her new sight. This was the Most Treasured of Treasures she sought in her stories.

It was in that magical moment that Meigga's hands rose as if compelled by some unseen force and swiftly, effortlessly raised the lid.

Inside was the Full Moon blazing in glory. Stars twinkled over its face. Still, they beckoned, as before they once had.

Dance!

~

*I*sabelle Merchant awoke to see herself sleeping, the legatee of Meigga.

The mere sliver of a crescent hung low on the horizon, yet somehow it blazed and lit Isa's face with a candling glow.

CHAPTER 51

*T*he sun was dipping its paint in twilight, brushing the canvas with uncannily vibrant pastels. An *umberish* red glowed like embers from the rocky peaks to the east.

Isa sat in the resort's open-air restaurant overlooking the rocky skyline. She was alone at her table with a Shirley Temple, her favorite drink as a child, and sat quietly entranced by the views as a warm gust swept in and feathered her hair.

She had crossed the sands to Arizona in search of escape. She'd come for the daytime sun to warm her heart, for the nighttime peace to soothe her soul.

Back home on the coast, the beach had always been her salvation. A place of retreat from the injuries of life. Isa would submit to the sun's saturation penetrating her skin, muscles, and bones deep into her very soul. Then she would immerse herself in the magnificence of the sea, surrendering fully to the surf as it kneaded and cleansed and helped release all her pains.

But none of life's hurts had wounded so deeply as the last. It was as if she'd been impaled in her core by a jagged, rusted blade, robbed of her breath and stripped of all strength. Her sorrow's rise to grief had come and then gone. But soon grief had come once more and stayed.

As she sat there she wondered, when again would it go?

"You seemed to be mesmerized by the view," a voice said.

Isabelle looked up to see a tall woman somewhere in her golden years with a serene face and cerulean blue eyes She had peach-colored hair and a kind, wisened face.

"I'm sorry to break your spell," she said, "but the pull to come over here was magnetic. My name is Ell. May I join you?"

"Yes, yes. I'm Isa— Isabelle. Please call me Isa," she stammered nervously, not sure what she was feeling or why.

"I was sitting over there," Ell pointed behind her, "and noticed something very familiar about you. Familiar—though I can't place you —and fascinating. I feel like I'm looking at a part of my younger self. You're strikingly beautiful. I once was too."

"You still are," Isa said with meaning. Ell's elegant beauty shone through the years. There was a regal magnificence. Beauty, charm, majesty. "You have an electrifying presence. It's a bit… *overwhelming*."

"Really?" said Ell as she sat down. The older woman's voice had a rich, dignified tone. "I feel that I know you, Isa. But how is unclear."

"Yes, I know. Me too," said Isa. "Your face— And your voice. But I don't think we've met."

"An aura of tranquility surrounds you, Isa. But I sense a deep sadness at the core. Like you've been weeping quiet tears." Ell leaned down to the bag at her side. Her hand emerged with a single, red rose.

Isa's eyes grew wide.

"I went to the market today and saw this. Not something I would normally buy. And this evening, I felt the need to bring it to dinner. I didn't know why then. Now I do. This rose is for you," Ell said, handing it to Isa.

"Oh!" Isa's round eyes pooled like an ice rink had instantly melted by the parting of clouds.

"Love never dies," Ell said, holding Isa's gaze. "Love *never* dies."

Isa stared through the stunned-blur of her wet eyes. When at last she spoke, she held the flower close to her nose.

"This morning I thought I saw a rose. It wasn't, though. It was a lotus in a pond. But for a moment it looked like a rose to me. I swear I could hear my mother's voice in the wind. 'Love never dies,' she said. But how could that be? Right? So I chalked it up to a wishful fantasy.

"But now you...," Isa shook again, the sadness moving through her in ripples.

Ell reached out to take Isa's hands in hers, clasping them in the warmth of her sympathy. When she spoke her voice was resonant and strong.

"Dear child, your mother lives. She is here with us now and wants you to know that her love for you will never die. She wants you to know that she loves you to the moon and back."

CHAPTER 52

*A*fter sharing a tableful of Arizona tapas, the new friends walked arm-in-arm to Ell's personal villa high atop the vast property. It was one of only a handful of privately-owned villas in the resort and sat on a cliff.

The main room was peppered with candles and crystals. A magnificent purple amethyst the size of a monk seated in meditation was set against one wall. Its brilliance anchored the space.

"This is lovely," Isa said, admiring it all.

"It's a peaceful home," said Ell. "My husband leaves me alone when I'm in need of isolation. He is traveling now, so I can write."

"You're an author?"

"I've been writing for a long time, but my first book is only now beginning to take shape."

"What's it about?"

"Freedom."

The kettle's whistle sent Ell off to the kitchen. Isa had no sooner sunk into the sofa when Ell returned with a pot of what smelled like chamomile tea and two large mugs.

"I can't begin to tell you how strange I feel here," said Isa. "It's as if there's something magical about this place. Like I'm in some kind of

Shangri-La. And now you. *Who are you?* Telling me things only I could know.

"Once— I was so little. I caught a starfish. And my mother told me she loved me to the moon and back. I'd forgotten until I dreamt of it last night. At least I think it was a dream. In the dream or the memory, whatever it was, my mother told me, 'I love you to the moon and back.' Just like you— *Exactly* like you said."

Isa looked straight into Ell's eyes. "I'm not sure I ever really knew how truly deeply my mother loved me till then. *To the moon and back.* She really meant it."

"She brought you that dream," Ell said. "She wanted you to know— to *remember*—how precious you were to her. Always. Throughout her life. Even at the end. Even now."

"This is all so surreal. I'm not even sure what to believe anymore."

"This is all very real," Ell chuckled. "I could pinch you if you like."

Isa chewed on her lip for a moment. "How can you know the things you know? I'd like to understand, but it's blurry for me. I mean, I know about psychics and all. But I'm still asking."

Ell smiled. "It's a great question. Such things are not meant to be a mystery. Some people are born with a clear connection to their inner voice. Some develop it through the course of their life, some not as much. It's a sixth sense that defies common logic and reason, yet it's still very real.

"Some are innately gifted with the ability to connect beyond the veil to those who have passed on. They're able to bring forth messages of comfort and hope, words of forgiveness and reconciliation. And yet the ability to speak to the dead, *mediumship*, is not the goal and shouldn't become the focus of such exploration.

"Few are aware that such abilities are only a glimpse of what can be experienced when we have truly understood who we are. Once we've chosen to embrace our potential. You see, the greater endeavor is to grasp more fully the true awareness of who we are as humans. Who we are and what our purpose is for being. Only then can we make sense of the chaos of life as we know it. As we integrate that understanding practically into our lives, we can make ourselves whole.

"You see, who we truly are when we are made whole is far greater than anything we can perceive at this time. Far, far greater."

"That's a lot to take in and..." Isa searched her thoughts. "I don't know. It's the stuff of fiction."

"The true spiritual quest requires the willing suspension of disbelief, just like all great stories. You must dissolve the boundaries of your perception. Set aside your beliefs, if but for a moment, to consider yet unimagined possibilities. This is the true freedom I write about."

Ell paused a second, then said, "Isa, I feel that you are also deeply intuitive. I don't think you even know how strong it is in you."

"My mother used to say that."

"You wonder how I know the things I know," said Ell. "Well let me ask you, how did you know to wake up just moments before your mother's last breath?"

Isa gasped.

Oh my God! Who was this woman?

CHAPTER 53

*I*sa remembered how Marie had fallen into a deep sleep in the final week of her life. Pain from her tumors had grown to such a crescendo that she was on a steady course of medications that left her completely subdued and inert.

It was an exhausting ordeal for Isa, each passing hour draining her mentally and emotionally. Physically, Isa swept aside her depletion, catching pockets of sleep whenever Nurse Wendy was there.

It was late one evening when Isa noticed her mother's face was lit by the full moon bearing down from the skies and in through the window. There was a heavenly calm as Isa at once saw in her mother the overwhelming beauty that she was. The ravages of cancer had stripped her of vitality, but on that evening Marie looked every bit God's angel.

Isa didn't leave the room that night and slept on the floor alongside her mother's bed. It was not long before Isa found herself stirred from her slumber. Something was different. What was it?

The rhythm in her mother's breathing had changed. Slower and softer. Isa rose and went to the foot of her bed.

Wendy slept quietly in an armchair just outside the room. But Isa couldn't move to call her. It was as if her feet had been sunk in concrete.

And there she stood, a witness to a sacred event.

As her mother's breathing softly fell.

Slowing evermore in cadence. Easing in depth. Ever so gently. Until it was nothing.

At that very moment, Isa felt her heart flip inside her chest. Pain, relief, and love indelibly etched.

Marie had gone home.

∼

"*Y*ou couldn't have said it better, Isa," Ell said softly. "Your mother went home. Not everyone appreciates that the veil between here and beyond is simply that. A veil.

"No one dies. There is no end, only continuation. And those who have crossed the veil are the ones who are home. Such folly our lamentations."

"Yes," Isa said. "But how did you know my story, that I woke up just before she passed?"

"Let me tell you that the impulse that awakened you to bear witness and usher your mother home is an example of the greater knowing that constantly guides us. Some call it instinct. Some call it gut or intuition. It is all of these things and still so much more. Yet so few are aware it exists. Even fewer listen when it speaks.

"You were susceptible because you were sleeping. We're more open to inspiration when in states of deep relaxation. And whether we remember it or not is often inconsequential. The idea or the thought—the seed of inspiration—will have been planted. And it will germinate in perfect time.

"When you are inspired as you were on that night, it is the work of a higher form of guidance you are receiving and heeding. In your case, it seems you've always had a deep connection with your inner awareness.

"You listened to the unspeaking voice as it guided you to sleep at her side. You listened when it was time to awaken. You listened when it guided you to stand at the foot of her bed in the perfect moment of life's completion and to lift your mother into the heavens."

"I didn't feel all that at the time."

"Understand that you were ready for her to go. And *she* was ready to go. Energetically, you did, in fact, release her in that moonlight moment when you truly noticed her beauty. It was not just her physicality you honored but everything she had been in her life. You honored the perfection of her being and blessed her through your recognition.

"And your presence helped anchor an energy of such powerful love in the room that she was gently lifted from her shell and into a vortex of love. In an instant, she was home."

"Where did she go?"

"As I've said, death is an illusion. It doesn't exist. Death is simply a change in energy, a change in *frequency*. Your mother didn't cease to exist when she set her body aside. No! She is a vibrant and unique being whose existence is not defined by the brevity of one solitary lifetime.

"To be more accurate, she simply slipped out of her earth-space-suit where the human spell of forgetfulness was immediately broken. She is still your mother and continues to wear the energetic cloak of the image she wore when she was in this world. Except that now she looks quite young, more like she did when she was your age. And her bond with you remains just as strong as it was in this world, if not stronger now fueled by the conscious fullness of her being."

"Is she here with us now?"

"She is. She's dancing around you blowing kisses as if she's sprinkling you with fairy dust."

Isa sat in the space of this experience for a moment, her emotions rooting deeper. Every word Ell had spoken echoed as truth in her heart. The company of this beautiful, incredible, strange woman and the words she'd just spoken now consumed her whole body. Isa felt she would burst.

"Cry, my child," Ell said. "Cry until you can cry no more. Don't muffle your emotions. Strength will come from this. More strength that you have yet to know."

And in that moment Isa could no longer hold back what wouldn't be held.

She dropped her chin to her chest and wept.

CHAPTER 54

*A*fter a time Isa raised her head to Ell.

"Do you still feel my mother?"

"Yes. She's here with us."

"Can I ask her a question?"

"Of course."

"A few days before she passed away, she was deeply sedated. Hadn't moved on her own in a while. All of a sudden her right arm lifted up. Her fingers could have been holding a pen. She started writing in the air.

"At the time, my mind was— I mean, I figured she was trying to write me a message, but the movements weren't forming letters. And remember, she hadn't moved. *At all! In days!*

"I didn't think to voice my confusion to her at the time. I don't know why. I guess I didn't want to distress her by saying I didn't understand. But after she died, I started wondering, what had she been trying to say? It's been haunting me."

Ell closed her eyes. She breathed deeply once and then twice. "It does have something to do with writing, but it's not very clear at this moment."

"*Me* writing?"

"No, not you. Don't get me wrong. You may be drawn to write one day. Don't hesitate when that impulse arises. But that's not what I'm feeling now."

Ell paused as if listening to a voice within and trying to understand. "Was your mother a writer?"

"No. She was a teacher. And she painted."

"I'm being shown a book. It seems to be hers. Written by her—"

"*Yes!* Yes. *Oh my God!* Yes, of course," Isa sputtered, her face lighting up. "My mother would read to me from a storybook she wrote when I was little. She made it for me. Wrote the story. Drew the pictures. Bound it in a beautiful leather cover she had embossed with all sorts of symbols. And the girl in the story had some incredible encounters with the moon— There's the damn moon again!"

Ell smiled, "It's important you remember. 'Remember my story,' your mother is saying."

"Okay. Yes. I have been. I actually remembered it this afternoon. Sort of. Dreamed I was in the story. Even though the story was different from what I remember."

"For now, you have an assignment. To grieve the death of your mother so that you can embrace her again as she is now."

"How do I do that?"

"You need to free yourself to feel deeply. Feel your regrets. Then forgive yourself. Weep. Miss her as she was so you can discover who she now is.

"Be open to triggers. Movies, songs, books. The goal is to *feel*. Whatever emotion that moves is okay.

"Remember your mother. And remember her story."

CHAPTER 55

*T*homas stirred from the deep to see Ariella place her hand on his chest. She wasn't timing his pulse, nor was she checking his breath. She was simply summoning him to wake.

She held an old tin cup toward him. "Drink from this. It will warm you," she said.

Thomas sipped the dull broth in the cup. Shadows of sadness peered back.

"You were dreaming," said Ariella.

"I need to go," he said, his voice breaking. "The storm, has it cleared?"

"You are in no condition to go. You are still in shock. Please. Stay awhile. Soon the storm will pass. You will feel much better and Gabo and I will help you from here. Not now.

"Please trust me. We have seen many such storms before. Do not despair. It will end soon, and you will be fine. Stay with me, Thomas. Do not resign."

And then she added, "Why not tell me your dreams?"

My dreams? Thomas's eyes searched. It might have appeared as if he was trying to piece them together, to make sense of the fragments, only to find nothing of substance to tell. But in truth Thomas was feeling conflicted, not knowing how much he should say.

"You may trust me," said Ariella, as if reading his thoughts. "My only wish is to help you. What do you remember?"

Thomas settled his eyes upon the fire in the hearth. As soon as he calmed, he felt the fire's warmth move through him.

"I was dreaming about things that happened to me just before I found my father. Not my father, but— Yes, my father."

A simple moment of silence passed between them.

"I'm sure he loved you more than life itself," said Ariella.

homas had hopped a ride away from Munich in a psychedelically-painted Volkswagen bus with a rowdy troop of young Italians from Rome who seemed to have come to the Olympics for no other reason than to drink beer and chase tall Munchkins in short skirts. *Munchnerins,* was the precise term, though Thomas's child-mind loved thinking of them as Munchkins.

The hairiest of the Italians gave Thomas his old Pinball Wizard t-shirt and a five-minute driving lesson before he climbed into the back of the bus with his friends and cracked open a fresh bottle of grappa. At the ripe old age of twelve, Thomas drove all the way to Rome with The Who blasting from behind.

On the outskirts of The Eternal City, they stopped for some gas. Thomas had been in the toilet when the bastards had driven off, leaving him stranded.

In Rome, Thomas made his life in the streets. He slept at night wherever he wished — offices, warehouses, even the occasional mattress shop. Before long, he learned that the best thing to do was to sneak into an inn a few minutes before eleven. It was the time of night that the evening shift was ending and the night shift came on.

In every modest hotel, the procedure was the same. The front desk clerk would meet with the night auditor in the back room and change out the till. While this was happening, Thomas would slip behind the desk, flip one of the room cards upside down and insert a maintenance flag into the hold. Then he'd lift the room keys and run.

It's not that he'd needed the keys. It was just as easy for him to pick a door lock. But he didn't want to leave the room key behind at the desk.

One time he'd been awakened in the dead of night by someone trying to get into his room. Fortunately, the chain had prevented their entry. Thomas had acted quickly. He called down to the front desk and—putting on the only adult voice his body allowed—screamed like a frightened signorina that someone was trying to break into the room.

The yelling scared the guests away, giving Thomas an opportunity to flee while the clerk was left trying to diffuse the storm and figure out what had gone wrong. After that, Thomas had always taken the room keys from the front desk. This way, there was little chance he'd be caught.

Thievery came easy to him. Whether it was a room key from reception, groceries from the corner market or tickets from the movie booth for the next day's matinee. He'd rarely steal cash because he could crack any lock and just grab whatever he needed. His favorite thing to do was to take a scooter for a ride around Rome. He'd most always drop it off within blocks from the start.

One evening, on one of his joyrides, he saw the same paint-splattered Volkswagen bus he'd driven from Munich parked at the curb near a bar. He broke in, got it rolling down the hill and popped the clutch to start the engine — another trick he'd learned on that trip.

Thomas drove around Rome until the gas ran out. Then he reached into his backpack and pulled out his memento.

The first thing the hairy bastard would see would be the Pinball Wizard he'd given to Thomas draped over the steering wheel.

CHAPTER 57

The joyride in the bus was like being bitten by a bug. After that, Thomas would regularly wake in the wee hours of pre-dawn when the police were half asleep and most *Romans* were snoring and sneak a joyride in some unsuspecting lout's fine automobile.

In order to avoid being caught breaking into the cars, he would light a number of firecrackers with very long fuses in different locations a few blocks away from his target ride. This way he was sure that anyone lurking about at that time of night would have their attention drawn far away from him when the explosions went off.

He never stole anything from the cars except for the gas, even when watches and wallets had been left inside. And he always returned the cars from where they'd been taken or at least close-by. His joyrides were harmless, juvenile fun. Yet driving those magnificent cars left him hoping that one day he'd have some of his very own.

One early-morning, Thomas was leaning under the dash of a rare BMW 2002 turbo as his firecrackers blasted in the distance when a man spoke directly behind him.

"This is one car you do not want to steal. Mafia," he added quite matter-of-factly.

Thomas was spooked and jerked his head hard into the steering column. His instinct was to run, but that's when he recognized the face behind the voice.

The first time he'd seen him, Thomas had been lurking in an alcove when he noticed someone walking down the road away from him. What caught his attention was the manner in which the man had rounded a corner — he'd suddenly gone from stooping heavily on a cane as he dragged his feet to nearly skipping as he swung his cane in the air.

He'd seen him again some weeks later. This time Thomas had followed carefully from the shadows and watched as the man again transformed, peeling off layers of gray hair from his chin and his brows and the top of his head to reveal the same bristly, short-cropped, dark mop that Thomas was looking at now.

"So, you are the friendly neighborhood car thief everyone's looking for," said the man.

"We all have our secrets, *Old Man*," Thomas said with a broad, toothy grin.

"Very clever! It appears I am not the only observant one here!" the man exclaimed and reached out his palm. "I am Esti."

CHAPTER 58

That day they laughed over a big breakfast at an all-night cafe, and when the sun rose they went to the man's apartment to drink more espresso. Thomas remembered being drawn into Esti's world. His home was full of canvases, paints, palettes, and brushes. Rags and turpentine. Thin white sheets that curtained the windows letting only light in.

That was the day Thomas's life had changed. The unlikely two—one just twelve, the other full-grown—had become instant friends. And soon much more than friends. In time Thomas had come to look upon Esti as the father he'd never really had.

Esti was employed at the Vatican, where he posed as an old man and wore the same disguise Thomas had caught him in. But his real profession was forger and thief. He'd create false duplicates of valuable paintings and documents then swap his fakes for the genuine art which he'd simply roll into the hollow core of his cane and carry out the gates.

"You'd be in a lot of trouble if they ever checked your stick," said Thomas.

"Not quite," said Esti. He reached for his cane and cautiously, methodically unscrewed one end. Tucked inside was a tiny vial of white powder.

"If anyone were to try to open this without following the right sequence of turns, the vial would crack and the powder would erupt into an intense fire — for only an instant but long enough to render any painting or paper inside to dust. There would be nothing in there to find."

"Groovy!" said Thomas, clearly impressed.

"When did you notice me?" asked Esti.

"When did I not?" said Thomas with a giggle. "The best time was when I was hiding behind a lamppost. I'd been following you off and on for a while. Trying to figure out what your game was.

"I saw a white-haired old man coming down the lane when a pretty girl walked out of a building in a waitress's uniform. I watched you transform to— well, *you* in seconds. You pulled your disguise off so fast that you forgot one of your bushy white eyebrows."

"Oh, I remember that!" said Esti, breaking into laughter. "I had no idea why she looked at me so strangely until I got home and went to wash my face!"

Gabo had joined Thomas and Ariella in front of the fire and was listening intently to the tale.

"Look at his eyes," he said to his wife. "They're dancing."

"Your eyes reveal much that is within you, dear boy," Gabo said. "Pray, tell us more."

"Yes!" said Ariella. "Perhaps something about this precious Bronze Globe I keep seeing."

CHAPTER 59

*B*efore Thomas could digest what Ariella had said, he found himself dreaming again — *remembering* again.

It was the middle of the night when Esti had awakened Thomas with a great roar.

"We are going to steal the Magdalene Treasure!"

And as simple as that, the greatest escapade of Thomas's life had begun.

At the Vatican, Esti had adopted the alias Niccolo San Tommaso. It was his old-man-disguise coupled with the sob story of his fictional wife's tragic death that got him the job working as a janitor at the Vatican Museums.

It also gave him access to Carlo Rinaldi, the curator who soon became his friend. Esti was older by just a few years, but Carlo didn't know that. Their friendship had grown out of the unreserved kindness that Carlo had shown him from the first time Esti had orchestrated their meeting with his tale of woe-for-sympathy. Carlo's compassion had touched Esti deeply and caused him on more than one occasion to question why he continued to deceive his friend.

But Esti was a dyed-in-the-wool thief. On top of this, Thomas had entered his life and quickly become his confidante and abettor. The young lad was sharper than he'd imagined. The result was that Esti was enjoying his work more than ever before.

Esti had quickly realized that Thomas had the guts for this line of work. After all, the boy had made his way on the streets in a foreign land at the young age of twelve. And he'd been surviving. Perhaps even thriving.

They planned their theft of the Magdalene Treasure for Monday morning. The Saturday evening before, Esti snuck Thomas into the Vatican to rehearse their steps, starting in Carlo's office where the Treasure was housed.

"How did you guys figure out how to open this thing?" Thomas asked as he examined the olive-tree engravings on the wooden structure Esti had told him about.

"I was looking for something out of place, however insignificant. Remember, it weighed much more than it should have. So we knew it was a container—"

"A puzzle box."

"Right. So I just kept looking until I found the trigger to open it."

"And the trigger is the crack, right? So you're the genius who found it," said Thomas proudly.

"Yes, I did," said Esti, ruffling the hair of his young friend. "Just imagine, it is from the hands of Jesus. Given to Mary Magdalene."

"And the manuscript?"

"Written by Mary, herself."

They'd almost been caught that night. Thomas was walking the grounds estimating how much time they would need to navigate a wheelchair from the Vatican grounds. Fortunately, Esti had been standing in the open doorway of Carlo's office when he heard the tell-tale click-clack of shoes coming down the hall. He'd been able to close the door and duck out of sight just in time to see Carlo appear with a beautiful woman he didn't recognize.

Esti had stepped forth before he could be caught lurking in the shadows. And then Thomas, too, had come running while he pushed Esti's janitorial cart as a stand-in for the wheelchair.

Thankfully, Carlo was obviously preoccupied that night with what appeared at the time to be a secret tryst in the making. Esti and Thomas had quickly retired for the night.

Never before had Thomas been involved in the actual act of thievery from the Vatican. Up till that point, Esti had always managed.

But on this occasion, they weren't dealing with objects that could be rolled into a cane or easily hidden on their bodies without alerting suspicion. So they had to come up with a disguise and a ruse that would conceal the Globe and eliminate the risk of scrutiny.

Esti hid in a Vatican broom-closet on Sunday night, just hours before they would exit the Vatican with the Treasure in tow. The next morning, Thomas showed up late.

"I'm sorry. I slept in."

"Better late than never," said Esti, stretching his arms wide in the cramped supply room. Then added wryly, "It gave me more time to nap on this stool."

Thomas put on his costume, dressing to look like a pregnant young woman, while Esti morphed into his younger self.

As they prepared to leave, Esti looked down and noticed Thomas's sneakers.

"You couldn't find something more suitable to wear?"

"Did you really think I'd wear women's shoes?"

"That was the plan."

"I told you no then," argued Thomas. "I wouldn't be caught dead."

"You might want to rethink that. High heels would do a lot to improve your popsicle calves," Esti laughed.

Thomas made a face as he took his seat in the wheelchair on top of the Codex's lead case, the flattened olive puzzle box and some papers Carlo had left on the table.

Thomas wore a scarf and large sunglasses to conceal his face, and over his T-shirt and shorts, he'd put on a long dress and overcoat to conceal the Bronze Globe.

"I'm going to die from the heat."

"Without the overcoat, you'd just be a scrawny woman with pipe cleaner arms. No one could ever believe I'd make you pregnant. Even now, I'm sure your baby weighs more than you!" Esti laughed again.

It when they reached home that Esti got the shock of his life. The lead case was empty. The Codex was gone.

He retraced his steps in his mind. But he remained convinced he hadn't left the Codex behind. He could think of only one possibility. Carlo and the woman in the shadows must have taken it.

Esti was surprised. It was highly uncharacteristic of Carlo, who'd always been very strict in observing museum protocol.

"What will we do?" Thomas asked.

"Perhaps we will steal the Codex from Carlo. It depends on what he does next."

"Will he get blamed for our theft?"

"We don't want that," said Esti.

It was at that moment that the seeds of intention were planted for a plan that would ensure that no one ever came looking for any of them. Not Thomas. Not Esti. Not Esti's friend Carlo. Nor Carlo's beautiful woman.

CHAPTER 60

*A*riella and Gabo were hovering over Thomas while he lay on the floor.

A smile crept onto his face as he remembered the fun that Esti brought to everything in life. *Oh, how he missed him.*

"What was the plan?" Ariella asked.

Thomas gasped — as he realized he'd not only been remembering events but *retelling* them too. He looked up to the faces looking down over him. The deed was done. The beans were spilt. But in his heart, he knew no harm would come from this now. After all, it was the caretakers who'd rescued him from sure death on the rocks. They were no threat.

"It was a clever plan," he started. "In addition to the Bronze Globe, Esti took some papers Carlo had left behind. They turned out to be the Gospel of J, which described the gist of the Magdalene Prophecy.

"Needless to say, the Gospel of J lead us to understand that the Magdalene Treasure was important beyond measure and transcended any monetary value we could conceive.

"We also realized pretty quickly that we couldn't sell or exchange it. The Treasure had already been kept hidden for centuries. And if we gave it back, nothing would change for centuries to come. We didn't know what we were going to do with it, but for the moment, at least we knew it couldn't go back. That decision changed the trajectory of our lives.

"Esti wanted to ensure we could never be pursued. So we knew we'd have to create confusion around our objectives. On top of that, we needed to buy time.

"'We have to make a clean escape,' Esti said. 'The only way is to give them the drama they expect and an ending they don't. When it's over, there should be nothing left for them to do but go back to their lives with their tails between their legs.'

"It was clear that Esti's career as a sticky-fingered cleaner at the Vatican was over. So we decided to take enough money to retire in comfort and safeguard the Treasure now and into the future.

Esti knew how to start a negotiation. "'Sky-high!' he said. 'We start sky high!'

"We planned early to get away with ten million dollars. That was the sum we needed. The rest was just part of the show. Esti was really a brilliant mastermind. He thought through every possible outcome of the scenario well in advance. He anticipated their responses and drew them right into the final act he wanted."

"Was it all Esti's plan?" Ariella said.

"Most of it, yes. But I helped him with everything. I played a lot with fireworks and balloons throughout the caper. And I stole the van and the scooter we needed — and used the scooter as my getaway when I took the ten million.

"Oh! And Esti asked me to devise a plan for delivering the ransom-exchange messages without giving us away.

"'Rely on what you know,' he said. 'What you're good at.'

"So I did. I came up with an amazing plan to shoot arrows into the Vatican Gardens.

"I never had so much fun!"

CHAPTER 61

"What happened to Esti?" asked Gabo.

A sudden wave of sadness washed over Thomas. "Soon after the theft, he started having heart problems. As time passed, they just got worse and worse. The doctors warned him he didn't have long. He was still young, but…

"I didn't realize at the time that he'd devoted the final months of his life to teaching me his craft— His craft as an artist, I mean. I grew up very quickly."

"It must have been hard to know you were losing the man who'd grown to become your father," said Ariella.

"Yes," Thomas said, unable to hold the rising emotion. "I remember the last morning of his life. I sat on his bed as he struggled to take in his breath.

"'Live well, my son. And care for the Most Treasured of Treasures,' he said. 'Follow your heart. It will guide you. Steal no more. You are an artist. Live your life as an artist. It was always my dream to do so. How often we forget to live our dreams once we have the means. Now you live them both for you and for me.'

"I was still just a kid when he died."

"And now? You have no family? No one special in your life?" said Gabo.

Thomas managed a slight shake of his head. He wouldn't speak of Yael.

"Why not, my boy?" the old man said with wonderment. "Tell me. Why not?"

"I don't really know," said Thomas.

"Nonsense, my boy. Everything has its reason."

"I'm quite happy alone."

"Really?"

Thomas's face softened in reflection. Suddenly, the image of a young woman with the delicate face of an angel appeared in his mind.

"Surely you have been in love before," Gabo prodded.

"Yes."

Thomas had recently moved into his new villa-by-the-sea, the same one he lived in today on Maddalena. One cool night under the light of the full moon he'd been planting flowers and ferns around a statue of St. Thomas he'd just placed in his garden. Off in the distance, he could see a beautiful young woman on a neighboring dock standing at her easel. She had hung a lantern to shed light on her canvas and palette.

From what he could see, she was painting a landscape—a picture of the moon shining down on a waterfall—that was curiously different from the one in her sights. He'd only been looking a moment when she too glanced over. Their eyes locked.

"I was a young man. But I was really just a boy."

"Who was she?"

Ariella saw through the silence that passed. "She was the only woman you truly fell in love with," she said.

"What happened?" said Gabo.

"I opened my heart. Shared all of my secrets. Then one day...," Thomas dropped his voice. "She ran out on me. Just up and left. I woke up one morning, and she was gone. With all of her things. No explanation. No goodbye. Just a one-word note that said Sorry."

CHAPTER 62

The Sedona sunset had ceded the stage to brilliant stars that now danced in the sky. In the hilltop bungalow, Ell watched as Isa ran her fingers over a tattoo on the outside of her thigh.

"What's that with the cross?" she asked.

"Oh, this?" Isa said, not realizing she'd been tracing the lines. "I like to think of it as the moon— *God!* Again the moon!"

Ell smiled.

"I got it when I was a kid. To cover an ugly scar underneath. I remember how pissed my mother was when she saw it."

"What caused the scar?"

Isa was perplexed by the question. "You know, I don't know. I— I can't remember. I fell maybe?" she said unconvincingly as she now stared at her leg. "I honestly don't remember ever knowing. It was always just there."

"What did your mother tell you?"

Isa sat dumbfounded, surprised by what Ell's questions revealed. "She never did."

"She wanted to talk to you," said Ell.

"About the scar?"

"Especially towards the end."

"Hmm."

Ell paused and then said, "She kept secrets from you."

"That I know."

"As you grew older, part of her just feared telling you what the secrets were. She didn't know how you'd take it. She had a very tender heart, your mother. She didn't want to hurt you. As time went on, she didn't want you to be angry with her, or disappointed, for not having said something sooner."

"This is heavy. I knew she had things she wanted to tell me. I remember there were a few times she tried. My sixteenth birthday. My twenty-first. As if the milestones made it important. But there was no way I could mistake the pain it brought to her. Like about my father. It was really, really hard for her to speak of him."

"What's your earliest memory in life?"

"Funny you should ask. It's actually a memory of a dream. Isn't that strange? I had an imaginary friend when I was a child. *Tello*," she said fondly.

"I dreamt that Tello and I were playing on a sofa in an apartment high over the city. Suddenly a VW Beetle came crashing through the large window in front of us. That was it. At least all I can remember anymore."

"And Tello?"

"Oh, I don't know. I don't really have a clear picture of him," Isa shrugged. "I just know he was my imaginary friend."

"Look again," said Ell.

"Hmm?" said Isa, not understanding.

"Close your eyes."

Suddenly an image of a little boy appeared in Isa's mind. He couldn't have been more than six, with dark, curly hair and the most dazzling green eyes.

"Tello?" she called.

The boy's face brightened, and his eyes beamed in delight.

"He's your brother Isa," said Ell.

CHAPTER 63

"*W*hat?" she gasped. "Tello was real?"

"There's nothing imaginary about him at all. You were just a little child when he died."

Ell paused just long enough for the words to echo in Isa's mind.

"It was such a tragedy. You can imagine. Your mother was distraught. Overwhelmed. It was almost too much for her to bear. If not for you, she would have fallen to pieces. She didn't know what to do. It was one challenge to cope with her own grief, but she also had you."

"Oh my God! I remember!" said Isa. "I can see him through my little-girl eyes. But his name wasn't Tello. It was... oh gosh... Fuh-tello," Isa said squinting through time's mist. "No, wait, *Fra-tello*. That's it!" And then she gasped and threw herself into her seat as it came together in her mind.

Fratello meant *brother* in Italian.

"He was your twin," Ell said.

"You know, I remember now. I have a memory of him holding my hand as I climbed a jungle gym on my third birthday. How could I have forgotten him?"

"He never left when he died. And you learned early on to hide his presence from Marie. Over time, he just moved further back into the corners of your awareness."

"But why? Why would I hide him from my mother?"

"Isa, your mother grieved for a really long time. The reason Marie didn't experience *you* suffering wasn't because you had forgotten him. It was because you hadn't *stopped* experiencing him. She saw no need to discuss his absence or his death. Because they weren't real to you.

"She'd watch you playing happily alone yet somehow with Tello as if nothing had changed. Each time she saw this her heart would break as if for the first time. She desperately wanted to see him, to speak with him, to feel him as you so naturally did. She knew that something extraordinary was happening, but at the same time, she didn't understand it completely.

"Although you were just a child, you felt her emotions deeply. I don't even think it was a conscious decision you made, but in time you found that by not playing with Tello when Marie was around, she wouldn't be so sad."

"He wasn't in my imagination?"

"No more than he is in this moment."

"I see his face," Isa said through soft eyes. "He looks much older than four or five, though."

"Yes. He's moved to an age where he's still a child yet articulate enough to be able to share the wisdom that fills him. He could have chosen to be any age, but eight suits him just fine. He enjoys being a little boy. Besides, it's easier for you to recognize him this way."

CHAPTER 64

"Why did Tello disappear from my life?"

"It was just the course of your childhood, Isa. As a young girl, your mind was largely clear. You lived in the moment not thinking too much. But as you got older and became busier with friends and with school, your mind also became busier. So there was less and less opportunity for him to pop in and spend time with you.

"But he never disappeared from your life. Never. He's always been with you. In fact, I see an incredible bond between you two that defies time and space."

"But I haven't seen him since… I don't know how long."

"Yes. But he's so connected with you Isa that he's able to whisper in your ear without you even noticing it. To you, it's as if you just had an idea or an inspiration. It doesn't mean that all of your ideas are his. But some of them are. Like the one that brought you here to Sedona. To this beautiful place. And to me. He wants you to know he helped Marie set this up."

"Really?"

"He says he's been influencing you forever. And since your mother is still getting used to being non-physical, it was a collaboration. He's saying that she waved her wand, and he made it happen. Your brother is funny."

Isa was almost giddy with a newfound joy that bubbled from within. Tello's face was still there, fully animated in her mind's eye. His green eyes intensified as if to shoot an electric pulse into her.

"He's trying to tell me something."

"What do you feel?"

"I don't know. I just see him."

"He's always been there in the Unseen. For all these years, you haven't had to know that he has been inspiring and motivating you. Guiding you. But because of the strong bond you two share, there is an opportunity for you to experience him quite clearly. You'll just have to give yourself some time to remember how to connect."

"But what's he saying?"

"Relax. And tell me what you feel."

Isa sat with her eyes closed, concentrating.

Finally, she opened them. "Nothing. I'm not getting anything. Can't you tell me what he's saying?"

"You *can* hear him. You've just forgotten how. Your excitement stands in the way."

"And my impatience! Please tell me!"

"He wants you to know that everything happened purposefully. His short time alive was meant to be. He says that because of the bond you had as twins, you two have never really been apart from one another. And this connection has served to hone in you a heightened sense of inner knowing. This will continue to develop in time. It will serve you greatly with all that is coming forward in your life."

Isa's gaze softened as she took in the message that Ell had conveyed. She lifted a knuckle to the corner of her eye to stave off a tear, then looked up once again. "How did he die?"

"You've stuffed the memory," said Ell. "Along with the trauma. Be with it. It'll come to you, Isa. But know one thing — your scar holds the story."

CHAPTER 65

*L*ater that night, back in her own room tucked into bed, Isa thought about what Ell had said. It was all so incredible. Mysterious. Unbelievable.

Isa couldn't deny what she felt was the truth. Her mother *had* guided her. Through the desert. Through her dreams. Through the lure of the flowers. Through the lotus-to-rose. Marie had brought her to Ell. And to the wisdom this great woman spoke.

It would take a great leap of faith, but Isa could see no other way for her. No matter how fantastical, everything Ell said resonated true to Isa's core.

In that moment, Isa remembered her mother sitting on the family room couch. It was a few weeks before Marie passed, and Isa had just returned from a quick visit to their school. Marie was completing a letter and put down her pen to give her daughter a kiss.

Nurse Wendy had been in the kitchen and leaned into the room. "How are you, Isa?" she said, but in her look was an unspoken *How are you coping?* The dear woman was tireless, never *not* thinking about the well-being of the people around her.

Isa smiled tightly and nodded. 'Thank you', she mouthed.

"I'm just going upstairs to prepare the meds for tonight," said Wendy. "I'll come and say goodbye when I'm done."

"I have some letters to be mailed out," Marie said, pointing to a short stack of envelopes on the side table. She'd undertaken to write a personal note of farewell to each of her friends. "Would you mind dropping them in the mailbox on your way out?"

"No problem. I'll grab them before I leave," Wendy said as she scooted up the stairs.

Marie looked up at Isa and patted the cushion next to her. "Come. Sit. That bag there— Take everything out."

Isa obliged her mother. She lifted the canvas tote off the floor and spilled its contents onto the coffee table.

"What's all this?"

"I don't think I've ever shown you."

Marie took a pair of thin, white cotton gloves that had been in the bag and slipped them onto her hands. Next, she had Isa lift what was left on the table onto their laps.

The first thing Isa noticed were the paintings and drawings — and the four tiny mountain peaks each one of them had in the bottom right corner. They formed the familiar *MM* of Marie's initials. One of the paintings was oddly foreboding — a pencil sketch of a haunting grey cloud in an otherwise clear sky.

"I had an envelope in here as well. Now, where is it?" Marie said, sifting through everything again.

"There's nothing left in the bag," said Isa. "Why the gloves?"

"I have a story to tell you."

The sun was low in the sky and through the window, its mirror could be seen glistening like jewels in the waves as they curled into shore.

The two women sat shoulder to shoulder, their legs folded, admiring Marie's art. Isa's favorite, also the largest, was of a magnificent waterfall pictured at night. The full moon reflected its brilliance through every drop that fell.

Marie held onto a portrait of a handsome green-eyed young man.

"God, he reminds me of someone. One of the boyfriends you never had?" Isa said playfully.

"We were so young. Together for eight incredible weeks. Then…," Marie sighed.

"Then?" Isa prompted gently.

"Then I left," she said, her voice cracking. Marie breathed quietly, collecting herself. Perhaps remembering. "Never saw him again."

"Why?"

"I was falling in love with him. And…" she sucked in a breath. "I became frightened, I suppose."

"Of him?"

"No, not of him. It's complicated. He was an artist. Not professionally, I don't think. I saw his sculptures, statues mostly, and paintings. He was quite wealthy. I assumed he had inherited money, but he never said anything about his family."

"Nothing?"

Marie shook her head. "Nothing that really told me anything about them. I did ask. But he just laughed and asked why it mattered. Then one night he shared with me his great, dark secret."

"What secret?"

Marie leaned her face close to Isa's and found room for a smile, "The Most Treasured of Treasures."

CHAPTER 66

"What?" Isa said after hearing Marie mention *the Most Treasured of Treasures*.

"You know," said Marie.

"You mean from the stories of Meigga?"

Marie's smile grew.

"Meigga's real?"

"Not her. The Treasure."

"You mean Meigga's wooden chest?"

"It was symbolic," said Marie.

"Of what?"

"He wouldn't tell me at first. Instead, he distracted me with this incredible story of how he and his father had orchestrated this amazing theft of two priceless objects from the Vatican Museums — and an even more spectacular getaway. I didn't know whether or not to believe him. The way he told it, I felt as if I'd been swept into the pages of a great Hollywood screenplay. It couldn't possibly be real."

"Was it?" Isa asked, unable to hide her anticipation.

"He put on gloves and refused to let me touch anything until I'd done the same. In fact, these are the same ones I wore that night. And then he showed me a stack of envelopes. I wish I could find the one I have. I'm sure it was here."

"It's okay, Mum. We'll look for it later. Tell me more."

"They were so decorative, beautifully addressed in broad calligraphic strokes. I almost expected them to be invitations to have tea with the Queen of England. And they had a bright red seal on the flap."

"What were they?"

"Ransom letters. To the Vatican. Their strategy was to send one envelope each day until they received a response. They were all addressed to the one Cardinal who knew what they'd stolen."

"Seems silly. Why not just send one? If the Cardinal knew the value of the art, wouldn't one have been enough?"

Marie laughed. "I asked him the very same question. The same question he'd asked his father before."

"And?"

"Do you know how many letters the Vatican receives in a day? Days and weeks can pass before one is opened. They couldn't chance that. A new letter every day that looked as magnificent as theirs would not go unnoticed."

"Sounds like they really thought things through."

Marie nodded, "They left little to chance."

"What happened next?"

"He opened one of the envelopes and showed it to me. It contained the ransom letter, sketches of the stolen items and another letter that someone had titled the Gospel of J. That's when I learned that the Most Treasured of Treasures consisted of an ancient manuscript and a bronze globe, together known as the Magdalene Treasure."

"As in Mary Magdalene?"

Marie raised and lowered her chin in a slow, exaggerated nod.

"What?" Isa exclaimed with her mouth as round as the sun.

"The manuscript was hers," said Marie. "The Magdalene Prophecy."

"You read the Prophecy?" Isa asked, finding her voice.

"I couldn't. He said that he'd just finished moving the Treasure to a secret location for safekeeping. But I did learn that the manuscript was written in Greek."

"Is that why you made me study that damn language?"

"It is," Marie twinkled. "But then you didn't."

"I took half a year," Isa laughed. "I might have stuck with it had I known why!"

"Not a chance. You're forgetting how headstrong you were. I should have told you *not* to study Greek. I'd have had better odds."

Isa laughed at the truth in that. "I was young."

"You still are, my sweet."

"So you never did read it?"

"Not directly. Some of the Prophecy had been memorialized in English in the Gospel of J."

"From the ransom letter."

"Yes. In all the years that passed, I've never stopped thinking about the vision it contained. It quickened my heart. I would have loved for you to have had that experience. It's why I wrote the stories of Meigga when you were a child. I wanted you to have a taste of my experience."

"Meigga," Isa said, remembering the storybook. "You used to read her to me all the time."

"The book is still on the bookshelf upstairs."

"What made you leave him? You said something frightened you. What was it?"

"My thoughts were a-jumble at the time. Everything was happening so fast. Unexpected things. I just had to get out of there. I felt scared — pure and simple.

"As exciting as it was at the start, soon the idea of having fallen in love with a thief from a family of thieves was too much. Not to mention what they'd stolen and from whom.

"I was overwhelmed. What was I getting myself into? I wondered if we'd always be hiding and looking over our shoulders. I just couldn't see myself living that way.

"And then he asked me if I thought that we might be the ones the Prophecy referred to. The *Two who were as One*."

"What's that?"

"Like the Chosen Ones."

Isa nodded mutely, recalling the stories of Meigga.

"The very idea jarred me," said Marie pensively. "No. It more than jarred me, Isa. It made me want to run."

CHAPTER 67

*I*sa tapped the portrait lightly. "Do you know where he is now?"

"I'm not sure. I know where he was then."

"And you never wanted to see him again?"

Tears appeared in Marie's eyes and quickly spilled down her cheeks.

"Once. It was very tragic what happened. You were so young," she stammered. Marie was trying hard not to cry.

It was a long while before her voice could be found. "I'm sorry, Isa, I'm so, so sorry I never told you," she said, with redness glazing her eyes.

"His name is Thomas Esti," she said, gazing down at the portrait. "Thomas is your father."

Isa had waited for this conversation all her life. Marie had only once spoken of Isa's father. She was about six or seven at the time. It was Father's Day and a friend had told her about the breakfast in bed she'd shared with her dad. Isa had come home from school that day just needing to know.

Marie had only gotten as far as telling Isa her father was a man of many talents — a sailor, an artist. Isa had used her imagination to fill in the rest.

For a short while after 9/11, Isa had taken to imagining her dad as one of the firemen who'd risked his own life to rescue the frightened people trapped in the buildings. He was a hero.

Isa had pictured this moment a million times, the moment when her mother would finally tell her about her father. And each time, Isa had imagined she'd be shocked senseless by the news.

But the reality was different. What Isa truly felt was deep heartache coming from Marie. She wrapped her arms around her mother, and together they cried.

"Can you forgive me?" Marie whispered after a while.

"Oh, Mum. Yes. Of course, yes."

Marie kissed Isa gently on her lips then wiped Isa's tears and took her daughter's face in her hands.

"Listen. You have to know that it was *after* I left him that I realized I was pregnant. Not before. It made me feel even more protective. How could I bring children into his world? For a long time, I was adamant. There was no way I'd permit it."

"And now?" Isa asked gently, earnestly. "How do you feel now?"

"I'm sure with the wisdom age brings I would do many things differently. But what does it gain to speculate? It can only cause regret.

"There were a lot of painful events in my life. I don't want to end my life holding regrets. I don't wish to be left with any hurts that I haven't forgiven, whether these were caused by me or by others."

"Dying changes things Isa. This has been my greatest gift, to have the time to go. Time to make peace. Time to find peace. I've come to see the futility of so many things in life— I mean things that are just not important.

"As I reflect on my life, the real substance that defines me is not what I earned, not what I've owned or where I live. It's the simple experiences I've had. The joys. The excitements. The love. Even my saddest experiences. They remain close to my heart. I wear all of them now like jewels on my crown."

"You've always been spiritual in this way."

"Is that spiritual? I'm not sure. Perhaps as I've become older. Now I look back on my life and I see the futility in every grudge I held. In not having spoken my truth in every moment. In not expressing myself freely to everyone, everywhere, all the time.

"I had a lot of fear, Isa. From my childhood. Things that overwhelmed me and created a pattern in me that became more habit than choice. And my habit was to withdraw.

"Somehow I found the freedom to be open with the children in my classroom. But it took me a long time to step outside that circle of safety. If I were to do it again, I would live every moment conscious of what's essential in life. Just being happy. It's my only wish for you. Maybe you will see life that simply."

In that moment Isa was seeing Marie in a whole new light. Her mother had become who she was through the trials and fires of life.

"I love you, Mum."

The conversation had taken a lot out of Marie, who was now leaning most of her weight on Isa.

Nurse Wendy crept into the room and went straight to her patient. "You look uncomfortable Marie. How much pain?"

Marie grimaced, "Seven."

Isa flinched. Seven out of ten. This is what her mother's suffering had become. Mere numbers on a scale.

"Let's take care of that," Wendy said and climbed back up the stairs.

Marie looked at Isa through crimson-lined eyes. "I'm sorry I never told you. I just couldn't."

Holding back tears, Isa pressed her head into her mother's bosom and hugged her tightly. "I love you, Mum. Nothing but."

Marie lay quietly on the couch after Wendy had given her a shot. A pain killer to kill the pain. Why couldn't they just mix something up to kill what caused all the pain? It all seemed so silly.

Isa gave Wendy a peck on the cheek. "Thank you for everything. *Everything-everything*. I'll be forever grateful to you."

Wendy picked up the envelopes Marie had left to be mailed and reached for another that had fallen under the couch.

Isa was in her own thoughts and hadn't heard Wendy nor seen that the envelope she'd picked up from the floor had a curious red seal on the flap.

"Your mother's a true artist."

"She sure is," said Isa, looking up. "Leave the envelopes on the front table, Wendy. You get home now. It's late. I'll mail them later."

CHAPTER 68

The lighthouse cast a dim glow on Thomas's face, revealing a dull, grey pallor.

"I'm really not feeling well," he said.

Ariella wiped the sweat from his brow with a cool, damp cloth she'd soaked in the essence of myrrh. "It's time to make peace."

"What was her name?" asked Gabo.

"Hmm?"

"The woman you loved so long ago."

"Marie."

"Do you still love her?"

Thomas hesitated as the realization sunk in. "Yes."

"Did you ever see her again?"

Thomas shook his head. "A couple of years later, I received a letter. She was coming to Rome and wanted to meet."

"At a park?"

"Yes. I was excited. Confused but excited. Unfortunately, there was a terrible accident that day. A train derailed after hitting a car crossing the tracks. There were dozens of injured and a handful who'd died.

"All the roads had been closed for miles all around. By the time I arrived, she was gone." Thomas mused, "Or she'd never come at all. Who knows?"

"I'm sorry," said Gabo. "It must have been painful."

"Twice she came into my life, raised my hopes then dashed them. Many years later I found where she lived, but it was too late."

Gabo drew close, and Thomas could smell the hints of cinnamon and clove on his breath.

"Throughout your life, you've carried the wounds of a little boy who was rejected by the ones who were meant to love you. Your parents scarred you horribly. You came to believe you were not worthy of anything good. Not worthy of being happy. Not worthy of being loved.

"That is until Esti showed you something different.

"Marie had her own demons to battle. And when she ran from you, it triggered your fears. Rather than chase after her on a white horse to the ends of the earth, you felt defeated. You took what happened with Marie as proof that you were completely unworthy of being loved. And so you buried yourself in your cars and your boats and your art.

"You missed out on having a great partner in life. A great love. A great family."

"Are you telling me my life could have been different?"

"Who is to say what might have been? Destiny tends to have its way. Your life was perfect," Gabo said cryptically.

"How can that be? How can my life have been perfect if I could have been with Marie? *That* would have been perfect."

"Paradox," he said plainly as if to explain. "It is just another of Life's mysteries you have yet to unravel. You will soon see the perfection."

Thomas fell silent. "I've never stopped wondering why she left. I was so deeply in love. I thought she was too. And then years later, why didn't she show up? She'd come all the way to Rome to see me and then—

"Why?"

Suddenly Thomas felt like he was watching a movie, and the world was his screen. He saw himself stepping into a red sports car parked in front of a hotel. He fired up the engine, raised his aviator sunglasses and peered into the mirror to check his teeth. He popped a mint in his mouth and sped out the drive.

"That's Rome!" Thomas said. "The day I was going to meet Marie in the park! How—?"

"Watch," said Gabo.

The movie continued. Thomas's view lifted from the roof of his sports car and across the city as a bird would fly until he could make out his destination.

There Marie sat on a bench with a sketchbook in hand. She was pencil-sketching one of the clouds in the sky. It had a core of deep grey.

"So she *was* there!" Thomas said.

"Look more closely," said Gabo.

Next to Marie on the park bench was a picnic basket.

"Mummy!" a voice called.

Marie looked over to a little boy and girl playing in the field and waved.

"Watch me!" the boy yelled and kicked a soccer ball as hard as he could. He reached for the hand of the little girl and together they ran after it.

Marie watched for a bit then returned to her sketchbook. She was shading some of the heavier lines of grey that darkened the cloud.

Thomas saw the two children again hand in hand, chasing another of the little boy's kicks.

Marie sat quietly, her head in the clouds.

Thomas's view now moved down the road to a Volkswagen Bug swerving as it drew closer, veering left and veering right. Suddenly, it jumped the curb, pummeled a mailbox into the sky and slammed into the two tiny children chasing their ball.

Thomas's chest tightened as if an electric chair belt had been cinched around him. The children lay meters from where they'd been — the girl knocked unconscious, a deep gash in her leg. The boy was lifeless beside her. They were still holding hands.

Thomas was flooded with emotions he'd never felt before. Such sadness poured through him, he felt he could drown.

"This really happened?" Thomas said, choking as he found the words.

"Five minutes later, the drunkard drove his car right into the path of a passenger train. That's what closed all the roads."

"Both of Marie's children died?"

"Your daughter survived."

"What?!" Thomas was agog. "Those were *my* children?"

Gabo nodded. "Twins. Isabelle and Nicolas. Marie named your boy after the father you'd told her about, Niccolo San Tommaso. So he became Nicolas."

"She came to Rome so I could meet them."

"She wanted much more than that. But the accident changed everything. It really was too much for her to bear. As a mother, she was overwhelmed with guilt for not having protected them. She didn't know how she could ever face you. It took her a long time to overcome those feelings.

"If not for Isabelle, Marie would not have survived. Or she would have dimmed her light so much that she might as well have been gone.

"But Isabelle became her world. Everything she did, every choice she made, was with her little girl foremost in her mind. And thus was her life.

"But you should know that she could never forget you. And she never stopped loving you."

CHAPTER 69

*T*homas was jolted by a loud sound he couldn't quite place. It was as if a large book had fallen to the floor with a bang. He shook with fright as he looked down at his battered body. Blood was now pooling through the blanket.

"Be calm with me this moment," said Gabo gently. "You have nothing to fear."

"Am I dying?"

"You are in my hands now. Many a sailor has been lost against these rocky shores. Many have I brought into this space to heal. Some were so gripped with fear, there was little I could do. But those who found comfort in my words lived on. Trust me, dear boy. Breathe in Life. I wish for you to live!"

"I'm not ready to die."

"There is no such thing as death, my boy. Only suffering can die. Life continues. You are not your body. You are more than you think yourself to be. You are a great light that chose this body for the gift of the life that it granted."

"I'm not me?"

"You are who you *feel* yourself to be and so much more."

"Am I going to hell?"

"There is no hell other than the one you would contrive for your own suffering. Why would you do that?"

"What am I supposed to measure my life against? How can I know whether I failed or... or succeeded?"

"There is no failure. And success is determined by how deeply you feel through the rigors of life. Only you can measure your so-called successes.

"There are no overall dictates that are set for humans to follow. To do so would abrogate the purpose of each individual seeking its unique journey to know itself. No single formula would accommodate the journey of all."

"What do you mean?"

"The only measure of a life is the wisdom that you have gained from your experiences. From what you have truly, deeply felt. Could you deem yourself worthy enough to be free? To be happy? To be loved?"

"I've done so many hurtful things. My thievery. My hate. I can't even begin to tell you how much I've..."

"Sinned?" Gabo said. "Much of what you lament happened when you were young. You were escaping the winter of an unloving household. Your thievery, as you call it, in Rome was an act of sheer survival. It is not as if you were spending your nights contemplating how best to destroy the lives of others.

"All of your choices were based on whatever understanding you had of yourself in that given moment. How can you judge yourself for that? At all times you were doing the best that you thought you could do. You were responding to the circumstances of your life — and even those responses were based on whatever subjective reality you were experiencing at the time.

"Everything you have said and done in life was done in the moment based upon whatever unique experience you were having, whatever unique emotion you were feeling, whatever unique memory was being triggered. So there is no need for regret."

"But I hated my parents— Not Esti. But my real parents. I cursed them and wished they'd die."

"So you did."

"What kind of a boy does that?"

"One who has suffered. What they put you through was cold and unfeeling and cruel.

"It is time to forgive yourself for the pains of your childhood. They who were your parents could never have loved you. Affection and kindness were not in them to give. Had you not left when you did, your lot would only have worsened.

"You would have continued to suffer in the utter bleakness of their misery. That anguish would have stifled you, eventually drawing you into that very same blackness that you so intensely abhorred. You would have turned into that darkened soul whose only escape from torment would have been to torment others. You would have become the creature who acts out the deepest, darkest compulsions of his own personal tragedy."

"If that had happened, if I had stayed and turned dark, would I have gone to hell?"

"We would never have allowed you to create your own hell!" Ariella's voice boomed out of nowhere.

And then suddenly she was at Gabo's side again. "Had you gone down that path, we would still at this moment be lifting you from your despair, from your fears and your regrets. We would be reminding you that everything that happened served the purpose of giving you the wisdom that comes from life.

"Wisdom can only truly come from experience. And as you end your physical life, you bring with you all the wisdom of your experiences back to your home, back into your whole self. Understand that absolutely everything that has happened in your life did so with purpose. Nothing has ever been without it."

Gabo continued, "If you had continued down that dark path, you would now bear the wisdom of what it feels like to be so completely devoid of freedom, happiness, and love. You would carry home the understanding of what it feels like to be filled with rage and hatred and despair.

"And even this would have served your own evolution. For it is not until you have completely known darkness that the impetus arises within you to powerfully choose for light."

"But you can rejoice!" Ariella said. "For it was not your choosing to go down that tortured path. There was a brilliant and clear inner voice that compelled you, an inner guidance that led you to choose differently for yourself. To act differently for yourself. It was not easy, but you found a way out of the chasm. You *created* a way out.

"Others in your situation may not have acted so boldly. Their fears might have overwhelmed any impulse they had for a better life, a freer life, a happier life. But you braved those fears and thrust yourself across the world to a place where everything was foreign — the people, the culture, even the language. And you survived."

"By thievery," said Thomas.

"You survived!" said Ariella. "When you stole the precious Treasure from the Vatican, you were responding to the direction of Esti, the man who had become a true father to you. He loved you as you had not been shown love before. There was little he could have asked of you that you would not have gladly given. So grateful were you for his presence in your life.

"And remember, he devised an exciting and dangerous plan. How could you not be a part of it? It was not even a thought in your mind."

Ariella's face danced in the light of the hearth's flickering flames. "This man Esti, your true father, is in truth a very old and wise soul. He might not have acknowledged that in his lifetime or even understood what it meant to be as such, but he had a deep and compelling inner knowing that guided him."

"He was a thief!" said Thomas.

"So? This wisdom we speak of transcends common sense and reason. And you have that same depth. It is what drew you two together. It is this deep inner knowing that you both were truly responding to.

"You see, it was your contract in life to carry out this theft. Have you not considered this before? The Treasure *needed* to be freed from its holds. It needed to be brought out into the world and away from the coffers of those who are not destined to fulfill the Magdalene's prophecy. And it took two brave souls with a loose sense of right and wrong and with enough wisdom to heed their inner voice to carry out their part."

"Did I fail by not sharing the Treasure with the world?"

"No, it was not yet time. Nor is it yours to do."

"I don't understand."

"You don't need to understand. You simply need to hear me when I tell you that absolutely nothing happened in your life without purpose. Hear me when I tell you that it was your contract, your agreement, to come forth in this lifetime and deliver the sacred Treasure from its stony walls.

"And now as your end-hour has come, again you have passed the torch enabling the prophecy to be fulfilled. You have earned your place in the clouds where you may joyfully watch the magnificent unfolding of our Lady's sacred vision."

CHAPTER 70

"What will happen when I die?" asked Thomas, now more a child than he'd ever really been.

The caretakers smiled. "Most people simply return home. They cross into the light— Quite literally into the light. There they are immediately greeted by angels and loved ones they've known in life who are already home.

"Others fall into slumber when they die. This can happen to those who have held a deep-seeded belief that nothing exists after death — or the belief that their unique self ceases to exist and is merged with a higher power. And so these ones literally sleep behind a powerful field of their own mental construct that denies the continuing life that surrounds them.

"But eventually, their shells will be cracked. They will begin to bend to the reality of their true existence. They will sense the presence of those who have come to awaken them to the truth of life everlasting.

"Others still fall in the space in between. Neither acknowledging their shift nor falling asleep. They believe themselves to still be alive in their bodies. It is for them an altered experience. Not quite real, not quite unreal. But because it is their constructed reality they craft all manner of justifications for the strangeness.

"They do in fact continue to experience everything in the physical world they have departed. But this experience is skewed. And on a subconscious level, they create a subjective experience of physicalness for themselves as if it were real.

"Sometimes, these ones are closed to the subtle presence of those from the other side of the veil who are trying to help them make their transition. So they go about living their lives, but they are like ghosts. Their experience becomes one of being constantly shunned and ignored by family and friends, not realizing that their loved ones simply cannot see or hear them."

"But won't they see their family and friends grieving? Hear their cries? Won't they witness their own funeral?"

"The mind has the powerful ability to interpret any experience subjectively. So if the resistance of the one who is in limbo is great, they will dismiss these experiences altogether or they will dismiss portions of it that would show them the truth of what is occurring.

"Too often they become consumed with guilt and anger and all manner of dark emotions that are all merely a result of the denial of their new state and a falsely constructed experience of isolation."

"I don't want that," said Thomas.

"We see that you don't," said Ariella. "Come, then, won't you join us? It is time for you to bare your soul."

At that, both Ariella's and Gabo's images began to lighten. Then glow. They were as one at that moment.

"We stand on the boundary of here and beyond. And come to the place from whence you came, that place of despair and defeat, fear and unknown, that desperate place from which your soul called out for healing, for some hope and some guidance, some way to light the path to redemption, to forgiveness and to understanding. We stand in that space to light your path home."

"Is it my time now?" Thomas asked.

They smiled, their kindness enveloping him.

"I'm not scared anymore." Thomas looked down at his bloody,

bruised and broken body. His words came through sobs, "Am I dying now?"

"Let us revisit the events of your day."

Their eyes pierced his, and in a moment Thomas was watching himself driving his Aston Martin. Rain fell outside as he raced around the bends.

Suddenly the phone on his lap rang. He reached down to pick it up.

It had only taken that one moment with his eyes pulled from the road for Thomas to lose control of his car. The left tires dipped into the gravel and quickly corrected, throwing the right fender into the rail. By now all control was lost. The car nosed into the rising cliff wall then rolled mercilessly sideways down the road.

There had been no sun in his eyes to blind him. The sun had been hidden by clouds. The rain-soaked hiker in the middle of the road now showed himself as he truly had been, without Thomas's distortions clouding his sight. Standing before him was Gabo.

"You came for me *before* the crash," Thomas said.

"It was done before it was done."

"When did this happen?" asked Thomas.

"Now."

Thomas looked down at himself lying on the road. Blood seeped from his wounds.

One final breath escaped through his lips.

At that moment, Gabo and Ariella stood before him in shrouds of brilliant light.

"We have come to receive you, my boy! It is time for you to return home."

CHAPTER 71

*I*t had taken too long for Yael to get the engine started again after Thomas had slammed into her Mercedes on Caprera. And by the time she got the old clunker moving, he was too far ahead for any tactical maneuvers to be useful. With the radiator shot, the engine's temperature rose dangerously high. If not for the cooling effects of the rain, the motor would have exploded with heat.

And if not for her sheer force of will, Yael might easily have exploded as well. But she was *driven* by rage. And she held her focus on her mark — not on the throbbing pain in her knee and her stone-pummeled face.

It took Yael all of her efforts just to keep Thomas in sight as he roared across the bridge back onto Maddalena and north away from the town center. He was obviously a very good driver. He knew how to handle his Aston, rainstorm and all.

But Yael's skills were superior. And even though her car was not, worsened by the beating it had taken, her advantage held, bolstered by a fury edging on recklessness.

By the time they reached the north end of the island, Yael had closed the gap. But then she quickly lost sight of the Aston again as it sped around an extremely sharp bend carved into the rocky cliffs. Yael slowed, knowing the old tires would fail to hold grip.

She steered carefully through the turn only to see the Aston out of control a hundred meters ahead. Yael dropped all her weight on her brakes. *Oh no! This can't be happening!*

She watched as Thomas's car bounced off the guardrail then veered hard into the face of the mountain, spinning and rolling and smashing its way down the road, shedding metal and glass all the way. The Aston tumbled to a final stop, wheels down, at the apex of a turn. Any vehicles coming from the opposite direction would have little time to react.

Yael stepped to the mangled frame of Thomas's car, broken glass crunching beneath her shoes. His fucking 100 mph mistake! There was blood everywhere. He was clearly deader than dead. Skull cracked. Body twisted and broken.

She scanned inside the wreckage for the off-chance that he'd been carrying the Globe or the Codex. No such luck.

Then she heard a metallic voice.

In the footwell of the mangled car, she reached for a damaged cell-phone. Through the cracked screen, Yael could make out the caller's name.

ALESI

A man's voice was speaking, "Thomas, are you there? Thomas? What ha—?" The phone died.

Yael's mind was racing. She needed a moment to settle her clouds. She walked to the roadside and climbed a large rock cropping out like a ledge. She crept to the edge and peered over. The flat face of the cliff dropped to the wild sea, which was throwing up huge sprays as it pounded the wall. Much like the tumult going on in her mind.

She would stand on this mount for the time that it took to steel herself once more.

The wind was strong and it mixed with the rain, punishing her stony wounds. Without warning, a huge gust billowed her dress like a sail. It continued, blowing and sucking in random bursts, threatening to lift her and carry her with. But she stood firm in her stead. She would not be moved.

Suddenly a shiver ran through her, and the beautiful face of Thomas appeared in her mind.

But Yael thrust it away. She would allow only one thought to drown out all others. Where was the Magdalene Treasure?

CHAPTER 72

The solemn man in the rented sedan breathed in the cool air that blew from the sea. It was a short drive from the San Diego airport to the jewel of the southernmost coastline of California, the town of La Jolla.

Alex Elibon stopped for an early breakfast before driving to the address written on the card. He parked at the curb and waited for the street to wake up. The house he eyed was smaller than its neighbors, but the lot was quite large. It sat on a rise, which meant it would have some of the best sea views on the street. A For Sale sign was staked in the lawn with a nice picture of a bright-faced Debbie Ashcroft.

There was no activity at the house. No lights on inside. The blinds were all closed.

One neighbor a few doors down came out of her drive in a Range Rover, three kids in tow. When she saw Alex step out of his car and walk toward her, she looked away, spun the wheel and drove off in the other direction down the street. Not such neighborly neighbors. That or he'd spooked her.

Alex went to the front door of the house he'd been watching and rang the bell. No one answered. As he walked back to his car, another door opened across the street. The bright face of Debbie Ashcroft appeared, and she quickly made her way over to him.

"Hi!" she said. She really was just as cheery as her picture promised. "You're out early."

"Good morning. Maybe you can help me. I'm looking for Marie Merchant."

"Oh," she said, her cheer interrupted.

Her eyes jumped to his car, then his shoes and his clothes. She was sizing him up.

"I flew in from New York overnight. I'm a lawyer handling the affairs of a client. He passed away recently and left something for Ms. Merchant."

"Oh," she said again, this time frowning a bit. Perhaps *Oh* was just what she said when she didn't know what else to say.

"They were dear friends many years ago. It was his dying wish that I come here myself."

That did it.

"I don't know what to say," she said hesitantly. "You see, Marie also died just a few weeks ago."

"Oh," Alex said. Now he didn't know what to say.

"I'm sorry. You've come all this way," she said. But just as she started to leave, she halted mid-turn, "She has a daughter, you know. I'm helping her with Marie's house. If you like, I can call her and see if she'll meet with you."

"Yes, thank you. That would be great. I'm Alex," he said handing her his card.

She took the card and studied it while her other hand held a cell phone to her ear. "It's going to voicemail," she said sideways to Alex before leaving a message with his contact details.

"It could take her a while to get back to you. With all she's going through, you know. Well— Fingers crossed!" she said, her cheer sneaking back.

CHAPTER 73

*I*t took Alex the better part of the day to track down Isabelle Merchant's address on Neptune Avenue in Encinitas's elite Leucadia neighborhood, a short drive up the coast from La Jolla. He pulled into the nearest space a few doors from the oceanfront home and looked up to see the front door swing open.

His breath was literally taken away when the most incredibly beautiful woman stepped into view. Her long, dark hair glinted with gold from the sun.

So this was Isabelle. She was what poets could only describe as *beauty beheld*. A chord struck deeply within and carried an echo through the chambers of Alex's heart.

By the time he collected himself, she was a good distance down the block and walking quickly. Alex got out and followed, not wanting to run.

A few minutes later, she stepped to the terrace overlooking Moon-light Beach and sat on a brick ledge, with her legs dangling to the sea. She gazed out at the sun as it drifted into the endless blue. Behind her, the moon was rising, waxing to fullness.

Alex made his way to the terrace and leaned on the ledge. He took in the ocean, then turned to look at her. He felt like a nervous teenager at a middle school dance.

"Beautiful, isn't it?" she said.

He noticed her eyes were like turquoise in the sunlight and sparkled unlike any he'd ever seen.

"Yes... Yes," he stammered, unmistakably mesmerized by her.

"I meant the sunset!" she laughed, slapping her hand to her chest.

Alex laughed quietly, unsure of what to say. If ever Aphrodite chose to return, it would be as the miracle he saw before him. Nothing less would be worthy.

"Were you following me?" she asked lightly. There was not an ounce of concern in her voice. She seemed to be so completely in peace.

"I— I'm sorry for your loss," he said gently.

She hesitated, studying him closely. "Thank you. Do I know you?"

"Alex," he said, taking her hand in his. Her skin was cool and soft.

"Isabelle," she said.

It was at that very moment that the last throes of a water-bound sun cast a shimmering light on her neck. Alex glanced down to see the top of a pendant hanging from a simple gold chain. The rest was tucked behind her shirt, but what he saw was enough.

Thomas had once given Alex the very same gold disk to wear around his neck, explaining that he'd crafted it himself many years before. 'It's heavy, but you must wear it always. It cannot be lost.' And so Alex had worn it obligingly, dutifully, ever since that day.

"Does this mean anything to you?" Alex said to Isabelle, as he pulled his chain from his neck.

She snapped her head back in surprise. "Where did you get that?!"

"From Thomas Esti."

CHAPTER 74

*I*sa's eyes showed her surprise before even her words, "You know Thomas Esti?"

Alex nodded absently, his face growing grim. "Knew him, I guess. He just died. Two days ago."

"Oh!" she said, the weight of the news bearing down on her bones. "He was my father."

Isa and Alex cast their eyes to the sky as the sun made way for the infinite hues of the night to appear. Time passed in silence as the sound of the waves comforted them both.

"Just before he died, Thomas called me. It was three in the morning in New York. I was asleep. I heard the ringing but it felt like a dream. When I finally woke up, I'd missed the call. I called him back but—" Alex choked as he spoke, the memory painful to relate. "Three minutes. I missed him by just three minutes."

Isa put her hand on his. "Oh, gosh. I'm so sorry. It's okay. We can talk about this another time."

"This can't wait, Isabelle," said Alex, his voice thick with sadness. "I called back and the line connected. He was driving; I could hear the engine racing. He was fumbling with the phone and then… He crashed!

"The sounds were horrible. Scraping and bashing. Metal crunching. Glass breaking. I knew it was bad. Right away I called the police in Maddalena. It's a small island, and everybody knows Thomas. I told them what I'd heard. They promised to send out patrols right away.

"It was hours before they called back. They gave me all the little details. His body had been found with his wrecked car on the north of the island. They said it looked like he'd lost control in the rain."

"I'm so sorry, Alex. I know how you must feel," said Isa with the heartfelt earnestness that comes only from knowing the loss of one's own.

"Me? What about you? Isabelle, I'm so sorry to bring you this news. I didn't know he was your father."

"Nor did I. Until just recently. I never knew him."

They sat side by side looking out over the midnight blue and listened to the surf. The ever-present, all-powerful surf. Unknowing of night. Unknowing of loss. Unknowing the pain that these two had suffered. Just barreling on, as was its purpose to do.

Alex fought back his tears, knowing that more sadness hid in their wake. Grief would just have to wait. His focus now was to honor Thomas's final wish.

"I need you to hear something," Alex said. He pulled out his phone and turned up its volume. "Thomas left a message when he called. I didn't realize it till later. I've listened to it umpteen times. Know it by heart. I'm warning you, it's not easy to hear. Thomas sounds anxious and scared."

Isa nodded.

"Alesi, it's me. I'm in trouble. She's after me. Yael. The woman I told you about. I'm hiding on Caprera. I don't have time. Listen now. Carefully. Remember what I told you. Go to Marie. You both have the key. Follow the clues. Together. Don't act alone. It has to do with the Magdalene—"

The sound of screeching tires in the background had clearly interrupted Thomas's thoughts. Isa could hear the clunk of a rushed gear shift followed by hard acceleration. Then Thomas's voice came through once more,

---

"Follow the clues!"

The sound of a collision ended the call.

"Oh my God!" Isa trembled. "Did I just hear him die?"

"No. Thomas said he was hiding out on Caprera. It's another island linked to Maddalena by a bridge. Yael must have found him. That would have been the screeching tires we heard on his message. I guess they crashed, and he probably took off again. Back onto Maddalena."

"Is that where he died?"

"Yes. Just three minutes later. When I called him back. That's when I heard the fatal crash. I also heard another car pull up right after and someone walking on broken glass. At the time, I was confused. I thought it might be Thomas. So I called out. It must have been Yael."

"So who is she, this Yael?"

"Thomas told me about her just a couple of days before this happened. He rang me that day with things on his mind. He said he'd met an American tourist."

CHAPTER 75

*A*lex remembered the telephone conversation he'd had with Thomas.

"She is such a lovely woman, Alesi. She saw my garden statue from the sea while sailing and had to get a closer look. You remember my statue?"

"How could I forget Saint Thomas?"

"I'm not sure if I ever told you, but my first thought had actually been to sculpt Saint Nicholas."

"Santa Claus?" Alex joked. "With Rudolph and the elves?"

"He's the patron saint of repentant thieves, you know," Thomas said seriously.

"Saint Nick? So now you're a crook?" Alex said, playing into the gag.

"Not a petty crook, Alesi. A genuine thief," Thomas said with an even more serious tone.

"I'm not believing you," said Alex, though his tone had grown sober.

"A lifetime ago. I stole paintings and art papers worth millions. *Millions and millions,*" he added pointedly. "In capers with my father who'd been thieving for years. I was just a boy."

Alex took the news like a child who'd just dropped the ice cream from his cone. He was shocked to learn this side of the man who he'd known *differently* for so long.

"There was one heist, in particular, a half-century ago. It was our last. We stole an extraordinarily valuable Treasure far, far too precious to return.

"My father died a few years later. Since then I have never been completely sure what to do with it. I grappled with right and wrong for so long. But rather than torment myself, I finally chose to follow my father's lead and simply hold onto it.

"I have always known that this could not go on forever. The time would come when a different course of action would have to be taken. We had become custodians, the keepers of an ancient, sacred legacy. My father believed we were charged with the duty of safeguarding it at all costs. We dedicated the bulk of our ill-gotten fortune to that very cause. And I've devoted my whole life to it.

"I have done my best to keep it hidden. And as long as I'm alive, it'll stay hidden. But when I'm gone, it will be up to you and Marie to decide the fate."

"Marie?"

"Marie Merchant. Together, you have the key to the Treasure."

"What Treasure? And who is Marie?"

"It's all written down," said Thomas. "Remember that envelope I had you keep in your safe for me?"

"I thought maybe it was your will."

"You already have my will, Alesi."

"Well, an addendum then. I don't know. But you told me to open it when… You know."

"You're meant to inherit much more than you realize, Alesi. It wasn't time for me to tell you before. Now I feel that it is.

"This is a lot for me to take in, Thomas."

"Rise to the challenge, Alesi. This is not about me. And it's not about you. It's about the Treasure. I have always known that there was something greater than life about it. Truly greater than life. As if it was governed by some divine form of magic.

"I've come to believe that my best intentions were always met with the right insight that led me to act appropriately. I trust that. And I ask you to trust that too. You and Marie will be guided."

"You're sounding philosophical. Actually, melodramatic! What on earth did you steal?"

"I won't discuss this until we're face to face, Alesi. It's enough for you to know that there's nothing in this world that I deem to be of greater value. Nothing at all. Not even my life."

"Why do you say that? Are you in danger?"

"If it was known that the objects still existed, then yes. It would be a matter of life and death just as it was in the past. But no one knows. So there is no such danger.

"That's not to say that this isn't a great responsibility— It is the greatest! And this responsibility carries its own measure of jeopardy."

"This is all very hard for me to comprehend. Can't you tell me more? What is the Treasure?"

"The Most Treasured of Treasures. You'll understand more once we meet with Marie."

"Where is it hidden?"

"Where no one would ever think to look. You hold one piece to the puzzle and Marie holds another. There is more, but we will speak of it later."

"This tourist seems to have spooked you. Are you sure she isn't a threat to you?"

"Yael? She hasn't spooked me. There's nothing dangerous about her. She's very tender. Like a bird with a broken wing. I never thought...," his voice faded here as Thomas searched for his words.

"She's made me realize I've hidden *myself* along with the Treasure. It's time to pass the torch. I can no longer carry this responsibility alone. I'll catch a flight to New York tomorrow night, and we can continue to California together."

"California?"

"To see Marie."

CHAPTER 76

"So Yael killed my father?" asked Isa, when Alex finished his tale.

"Thomas said in his message from Caprera that he was hiding from her," explained Alex. "*Fleeing* from her, from the sound of it."

"You think she knows about the Treasure?"

Alex shrugged. "I really don't know what to think."

"But you and my mother both have the key. Isn't that what Thomas said?" Isa was fingering her pendant.

Alex nodded. "But the key to what?"

"You don't know what the Treasure is?"

Alex shook his head.

"Really? I do," said Isa, watching closely as Alex's eyes grew. "The Magdalene Treasure. An ancient Bronze Globe and a Codex."

Alex looked confused.

"How—" he started.

"My mum told me. And it's written on my locket," she said.

"What? What's written?" he said, finding his voice.

"Here," Isa said, pulling the chain from her neck. "On the outer edge of the face. I bet it's on yours too."

"The border?" Alex pulled off his pendant and studied it too. "Mine seems to have the same pattern."

"It's more than a pattern. It's an inscription."

"I never noticed it before."

"Mine says, *Key to the Most Treasured of Treasures*. You know what that is, right? The Magdalene Treasure."

Isa took hold of Alex's pendant and squinted. "Do you have your cellphone handy?"

She placed Alex's pendant on her lap and hovered his camera zoom over top. "There. See? *Key to the Most Treasured of Treasures*."

"What's that in the middle?" said Alex.

"St. Thomas." Then she looked up in disbelief. "Have you never studied your pendant before?"

He hadn't. But it didn't matter. Because Alex's mind was spinning, and things were quickly beginning to click.

"Isabelle— That image. It's not *just* St. Thomas. It's exactly the same as the statue of St. Thomas that *our* Thomas, your father, has at his home in Maddalena!"

"The same statue that Yael said she saw from her sailboat?" Isa said.

Alex nodded slowly. "That's the giveaway. Yael *must* have been after the Treasure. Thomas hadn't seen it."

"What do we do now?" said Isa.

"Exactly what your father said. Follow the clues."

"Yes! And we watch out for Yael!"

CHAPTER 77

*A*s Isabelle and Alex crossed high over the Atlantic to Barcelona, Isa toyed with her locket.

"I studied the engraving after my mother passed and realized it was St. Thomas by the carpenter's square in his hand. Then when I read about him and how he's represented in art, I realized that what I thought was a ribbon or a loop was the girdle of Mother Mary."

Alex chuckled, "With all due respect, I can't imaging Mother Mary wearing a girdle."

"A girdle is what a belt used to be called."

"At least in the old days anyway," said Alex, still grinning.

Isa rolled her eyes. "So you never drew the connection between the image on your pendant and Thomas's statue?"

"Well, not till now. It's so small. I don't remember ever noticing it."

"Not very observant. Are you?"

"Not some things, I suppose. Other things, I notice," he said, looking into her eyes.

Isa looked back, not hiding her feelings. She was equally intrigued by this beautiful man.

She reached for the chain around his neck. "The gemstones are different."

Embedded in the outer face of each of their pendants was a single jewel.

"Black and green," said Alex.

"Mine's a black sapphire. I think yours is an emerald," she said.

"What else have I missed?"

"I've always wondered about this," she said, raising his pendant up to his nose so he could see. She twisted the bale the chain snaked through ninety degrees. It released the hidden-clamshell's inner clasp and opened the pendant.

"I never knew!" said Alex.

"That it was a locket? I guessed as much. You're not very observant," she quipped.

Isa unfolded it completely. Three hinges connected the locket's cover to intricately-designed narrow gold fingers.

"Mine's the same. But I've studied it up and down, and I have no idea what to make of it. You should take a look. It must be a clue."

Alex took his pendant and its foldable links and studied them. He toyed with the gold, gradually exerting more and more pressure.

"This isn't pure gold," he said. "It seems to be an alloy designed to be much stronger. And not brittle. See? Look at this, I can extend the links and twist it like a screwdriver and it doesn't give at all. It's brilliantly crafted. Even the hinges."

"Look here," she said, holding up the four links. "What do you see?"

"Not sure."

"There. See? In the outline of the links."

Alex squinted.

"Look at the shadow it casts," she said, indicating the shade on her shirt. She slowly turned the pendant's links so that different angles became clear in the shadow. "It's St. Thomas again. He's carrying arrows on his back."

"Oh! I see it. The statue is everywhere!"

"But mine's a little different," said Isa. She'd opened her locket and held it against Alex's. See here? Yours has Mary's girdle pinned to the left side of his chest. Mine has it on the right."

"Another clue?"

"Don't know," she said, though her thoughts were very much focused on figuring it out.

"What shall we do when we reach Maddalena?"

"Follow the clues. We go to the statue first. Then we trust that we'll know what to do next."

CHAPTER 78

*A*lex and Isa were in a speedboat Alex had plucked from the docks in Barcelona. It was sleek and plush and rippingly fast. Isa had been strapped into her seat, enjoying the thrill, while Alex had piloted them expertly across the great sea to Maddalena.

Now they floated just offshore with all of their lights off. Alex peered through binoculars at Thomas's estate.

"How did you manage to arrange for this… this missile so quickly?" Isa asked.

"No arranging required. We own the boatyard. And half of the boats."

"We?"

"Thomas and me," Alex said, still scanning the shore. "The property is completely dark. Not a single light on anywhere. And I see no movement."

"You think it's safe?"

"I have to try," Alex said as he steered the boat towards Thomas's dock. "Just in case, you wait here—"

"No way!" Isa said firmly. "We do this together. It's what Thomas would want. You're standing in for him. I'm here for Marie.

"Besides, if anyone's there, they'll be at the house. We just need to get to the statue. You said it was hidden from the rest of the property."

Alex thought this through. She was right. They just needed to climb to the cluster of pines where the statue was. It was ringed in seclusion so there was little chance they'd be seen.

"Alright," he said.

"Don't pretend you have a choice," she retorted.

Alex cut the speedboat's motor while they were still far enough out that any noise would be lost to the sea. The momentum carried them in quietly. He expertly spun the boat at the last minute to bring it to a crawl — and also point it out to sea in case they'd need a hasty escape.

Alex jumped off and in rapid-succession tied a rope to the dock, peeked into the boathouse and peered over the rooftop's parapet.

"The coast is clear."

"Literally," Isa said.

Together they climbed the broad, stony steps cut into the hillside then veered off from the path that led to Thomas's main house. Isa could clearly make out a circular grove of pines. The section that faced the sea was sparsely treed, creating more of a horseshoe shape than a ring. As they entered, Isa could see an inner garden. And there in the very center was the statue of St. Thomas.

"There has to be a clue somewhere," Alex whispered. He tried everything he could think of to reveal something on the statue. But the head didn't spin. The hand didn't lift. And the kneecap wouldn't budge. Nothing moved.

Isa took a more thoughtful approach. She stood back and examined every inch of the bronze figure.

"It's beautiful," she said.

"Thomas sculpted it."

"Mum told me he was an artist."

"It wasn't his occupation. More of a hobby. But he did sculpt some statues for the island's town center."

"Look on his back. Those aren't spears like I thought. It's a quiver with four arrows— Oh! And here— Look!" said Isa, keeping her voice as low as her excitement would permit. "On his wrists."

The images were easily overlooked because of how faintly they'd been engraved. The right wrist rendered the planet. On the left wrist was a book with minute symbols etched on its cover.

"I was right," said Isa. "The Bronze Globe and the Codex."

"The Magdalene Treasure," said Alex.

CHAPTER 79

*I*sa's eyes fell now to the front of the statue. "What's this?" Her fingernail pierced a small aperture where the saint's heart would have been.

"I'm not sure."

Alex shined his flashlight inside, then pulled out his utility knife and probed.

Isa's voice punctuated the quiet. "Remember what Thomas said. You have the key to the Most Treasured of Treasures. He also said that we *both* have the key."

She opened her locket and unfurled the chainlink saint. "There may be another clue we haven't—"

"There's no clue, Isa." Alex's eyes were bulging. "*That's* the key!"

Isa looked puzzled.

"I mean literally. It's a key. Look at it. I mean it's far more intricate than a conventional key. God, it would be impossible to duplicate. But see here. The locket is the head of the key. The blade and bits are the chain links when they're fully extended. They may swing freely on the hinges, but when inserted into a lock, it won't matter. It'll still turn solidly."

Alex took Isa's locket-key and fed it into the opening on the statue. It fit perfectly. But the key didn't turn.

"Damn it," said Alex under his breath.

"Wait. Slow down. You're not wrong. Try again. But with *your* key. Remember, they're different."

In one seamless move, Alex pulled off his pendant, opened it and pushed it into the opening. His key slid into the aperture perfectly. He turned it with equal ease until they both heard a click. A narrow, rectangular panel popped open above the keyhole.

A heavy, concealed hinge sat on the inside of the panel door, along with two delicate glass vials. The space within resembled the cavity that a bank's safety deposit box slid into. Inside that space was a rolled-up canvas. As Isa reached for it, her hand brushed against the panel-door, dislodging one of the vials.

Isa shrieked as Alex unexpectedly spun her out of the way. The vial fell to the ground and a brilliant flash of light and smoke erupted. The patch of grass at their feet was now coal dust. Even the pebbles looked charred.

Alex pointed to the remaining vial. A skull-and-crossbones was painted on the end.

"Guess I didn't see that," Isa said sheepishly.

"This is some nasty concoction. The canvas would have been destroyed if we had forced open the door," said Alex.

"Why would Thomas do that?"

"I guess he couldn't risk having this fall into the wrong hands."

"Let's take a look," Isa said as she reached inside.

Alex held the flashlight while Isa unfurled the canvas. They found themselves looking at an intricate painting of a magnificent olive tree.

"A clue to another statue?" said Isa. "Did Thomas sculpt any trees?"

Alex's jaw dropped as his eyes turned to Isa. "Thomas's gift to the town. One of the statues is a fountain. Sculpted to resemble an olive tree."

"Let's go," said Isa, pushing the panel-door shut. "We follow the clues."

At the top of the hill, Alex entered his birthday into the pin pad of Thomas's garage. He pulled the door open then halted mid-step.

"What is it?" asked Isa.

"His Aston. It's gone. He must have been driving it."

Isa pulled Alex into her embrace. It was the first time she'd held his body so closely.

They stood awhile, as he gripped her tightly. Then he stepped back. "Thank you. I'm okay. Let's go."

He opened the passenger door of Thomas's new Range Rover and waited as Isa climbed in. Then he hopped into the driver's seat. The fob was in the center console. Alex slid it into his pocket as he clicked open the overhead door and fired up the engine.

CHAPTER 80

People were milling about in the center of town. It was still early in the evening, despite the darkness.

Isa and Alex made their way over to the plaza and stood before the bronze olive tree that had been so beautifully crafted. They rounded it several times but nothing stood out.

Isa shook off her shoes and climbed into the pool beneath the tree with a little girl and boy who were frolicking about. Alex followed, looking high while Isa looked low.

"This is huge!" she said. "How on earth are we going to find the keyhole?"

They both stepped out of the water and sat on a bench.

"Maybe there's a clue on the painting," said Alex, reaching for the canvas.

They studied it intently.

"Look at this." Alex pointed to the base of the olive tree's trunk. "This tree is different. See?"

Isa stared at the painting. "The base of the trunk looks like two trees entwining as one. Definitely not the same. Did Thomas sculpt another tree?"

Alex shook his head slowly as delight slowly brightened his face.

"What?" she said.

"Come on. It's not far."

Alex steered the Range Rover away from the town of Maddalena to the center of the island where an arboreal forest of pines rose majestically in the night. He parked at the roadside and pulled a utility kit from the rear. A flashlight guided the way.

Isa and Alex trekked a short distance until they came upon a small clearing. There in the middle was the very same olive tree that Thomas had painted onto the canvas.

"It's magnificent!" said Isa.

"Around a thousand years old. Thomas brought me here just once. Called it a treasure. Now I get what he was saying. He told me he wanted to preserve it at all costs. This property is a private nature reserve owned by one of Thomas's nameless companies, which by the way also has holdings in Los Angeles. Your neck of the woods."

Isa took hold of the flashlight and studied the tree. "It's difficult to see much in this light. But then I'd be hard-pressed to believe a living tree would have a keyhole in it."

She reached for the painting which was slung on her back like the roll of an architect's plans.

"Back to the clue."

Even in this light, they could see that the painting was a beautiful work of art. It showcased the olive tree in all of its splendor beneath a grey, cloudy sky. Thomas would surely have toiled for weeks if not months to achieve this degree of definition and artistry.

"What do you see?" asked Isa.

"This is definitely the same tree."

"So we're at the right spot…" Isa broke off as her eyes searched for some telltale sign.

Alex was pointing the flashlight all over the tree and the ground it occupied. The task was daunting, made worse by the darkness of night. He looked at her and shrugged.

"Where do we start?"

"Just look for something that stands out."

Both sets of eyes fell to the painting and followed Isa's lead as she moved her torchlight slowly over its surface.

"There seems to be shade everywhere except here." Isa pointed to one particular spot on the canvas where lavender grew as if out of a distinctly-shaped rock beneath the branches of the tree.

"Very interesting how he's painted it. Like a tangled vine."

But Alex saw more and laughed.

"Oh, Thomas! You clever man. See this?" he said to Isa, tracing his fingers over one of the vines that lay on the rock.

"What is that?"

"It's two E's in cursive. Our company logo for *Esti and Elibon*."

"Esti and Elibon?" Isa giggled. "Sounds like an Italian boy band."

"Something like that," Alex deadpanned.

"There's the rock," said Isa, pointing to the ground at her feet.

Alex lifted it up. There were no keyholes, no hidden compartments.

Isa scanned back and forth between the rock and the painting. "There's a pattern on the side of both rocks. See here," she pointed.

Engraved into the stone were three distinct symbols — a teardrop sandwiched by two notched lines that were inverse reflections of each other.

"That's not random," Isa said.

"No. It's a clue."

"As if that wasn't already obvious! This whole affair is one big puzzle," she said with big bugged eyes. "Back to the stones, now. It looks like arrows. One pointing up, the other one down."

"Or left and right, depending on how we hold it," said Alex.

Isa grunted. "I think we'd better stick with how we found it. And how it's shown in the painting. Up and down. Otherwise, the possibilities are infinite. The question is, what does it mean?"

"Well, above where the rock sat is the tree." He shined the light. "Nothing there but tree parts."

"And below?" said Isa.

Alex crouched down and dug his fingers through the soil where the stone had been, then drilled his pen even deeper.

"Nothing's here," he said.

"What's that notch in the middle? Looks like a raindrop," she said. "Or an apostrophe."

"Or the symbol for a minute," he mused. "Or a foot."

"And the arrows could be Ones. A right-side-up One, followed by an upside-down One."

"Or all of the above!" Alex sputtered, piecing it together. "A number, a symbol, and an arrow! One Foot Down!"

Alex dropped again to his knees and opened the Range Rover's kit. Any tool would do. He dug into the soil where the rock had been. Exactly one foot down the lug wrench hit metal.

As Alex cleared the dirt from the edges, he could see it was the lid of an elaborate bronze vault. But try as he might, there was no moving it.

"The tree might be easier to lift," said Alex with a tired grin.

"Maybe it won't matter," said Isa. "Look there. On the left side of the plaque."

Alex peered into the hole where Isa's finger pointed. On the top surface of the vault was a small circular plaque with the same arabesque floral design as the vines in the painting.

"The boy band," Isa said. "Esti and Elibon."

It took no more prompting than this. Alex toyed with the disk until it finally twisted on its invisible pivot to reveal a hidden keyhole.

Without a word, Isa knelt down and inserted her key snugly into the lock. She paused to whisper a silent prayer before she turned the key.

The lid released with a click. It was extremely heavy, like a small manhole cover. Alex took over and grappled while he figured out how to angle it up and out of the hole.

Inside the open vault was a single brick made entirely of glass. He pulled it out of the ground and handed it to Isa.

Encased within it was a very old leather-bound book.

Isa flooded with emotion as she remembered what she'd been told. It could only be the same ancient manuscript Thomas had stolen.

The Magdalene Prophecy.

CHAPTER 81

They sat at a cafe in the heart of Maddalena's brick-and-stone town center and studied the glass block.

"Thomas must have taken great pains to craft this just so," said Alex. "See inside the brick, near the book's spine? Another two vials of that powder. We can't risk exposing those chemicals. The glass creates a perfect seal. No air in or out."

"So then how will we get the Codex out without triggering the chemicals?" said Isa.

"We'll need a controlled environment in which we create a vacuum to draw out all air. The problem is that we'd then need to break the glass. Doing so, even inside a vacuum, would probably shatter the vial. And I have no way of knowing what would happen next. This one's tricky."

"There might be an easier way," said Isa. "He left us a clue."

On the brick's surface, Thomas had etched an intricately patterned geometric border and in the very center in bold script the words,

RAIN-LOOSENED CLOUDS
SET FREE THE SUN

"What does that mean?" said Alex.

Isa stared at the brick for what seemed to be a really long time then raised her blank face to meet Alex.

"Is that a shrug I see?" he smirked.

"It's a *Hell if I know!*" she said and laughed. "I'm out of ideas."

They sipped classic chianti and snacked on fragrant fruit, pungent cheese, and crusty bread. And while they ate, Alex's eyes kept dancing over Isa's face.

For Isa, it was amazing to think they were on the other end of the ocean together. They'd just met and yet...

The circumstances made it possible. Death had brought them together. For Isa, the loss of her mother. For Alex, the loss of Thomas.

Isa couldn't have comprehended the impact before it happened. But the moment it did, she understood completely. The need for connection on a very deep level. *The need and the willingness.* And she knew without asking that it was the same for Alex.

They couldn't have come together at a more perfect moment. Each one was exactly what the other needed. Marie had always said that blessings come in all forms.

"I can't imagine what would have happened if I hadn't found you," Alex said as if reading her thoughts.

"Funny that," she said with a gentle smile.

"Think about it. I didn't even know this thing was a locket," he said, pulling on the chain around his neck. "Let alone that it was inscribed. That it was Saint Thomas. That it was made in the perfect likeness of the statue. I mean, without you I wouldn't even have made it out of the starting gate."

Isa smiled. "Alex, you couldn't *not* have found me. My mother always said there was magic afoot in this world, things occurring that were beyond our understanding.

"What has happened here with us is not chance or happenstance. It's the unfolding of a greater plan. And Ell recently renewed my belief in this truth."

"I want to meet her. I'd love to get a message from the other side right about now." Alex's gaze had turned inward and a deep sadness showed on his brow.

"You okay?" Isa asked.

"I keep wondering what Thomas would have said to me if we'd had more time. What I would have said to him, given the chance. If we'd known, I mean, that his time…" he sighed. "Maybe things we'd never thought to say before."

Isa felt Alex's grief. The strain of all he had been through was wearing thin now.

"I miss him," said Alex. "And I feel foolish— I mean, he was your father after all."

"You knew him. I never did."

"It's selfish, I know. But, if I could just speak with him again. Just once more."

"And you wonder what Ell might have to say."

"Yeah," he said, without any wind in his breath.

"First she'd tell you to let it all out. To cry till you can cry no more. And—"

But before she could finish her thought, Alex squeezed his eyes shut. He dropped his face in his hands and wept.

CHAPTER 82

*I*t was as if her permission was all that Alex had needed. Isa watched as he quietly let grief pour down from his face.

When his tears had finally been spent, he slowly lifted his eyes to Isa. Beautiful Isa. The only one who could possibly know how he felt.

But Isa was staring closely at the painting.

"Here-here-here," she pointed to the grey clouds before Alex could ask. "Where your tears fell. See? The paint is running."

"I see—"

"But it can't. Acrylic doesn't bleed."

"What—"

"The clouds are water-based paint. *The clouds!*"

"Oh—"

"Yes!" she said, splashing more water from her glass. "Look again at what's inscribed on the brick. *Rain-loosened clouds set free the sun.*"

As she said it, Isa lifted a corner of the tablecloth and gently wiped the painted clouds in slow, circular motions until they disappeared. Where they had been, the sun shone brightly in a now-cloudless blue sky.

And written in fine blood-orange paint on the face of the sun she'd set free was their next clue.

~

*W*alking side by side, Isa and Alex wound through the magnificent stone streets of Maddalena's old port area. The latest clue seemed the most elusive of all.

The heart of the Magdalene bears the Light of this World

What was Thomas trying to say? It didn't seem possible that they could ever begin to comprehend Mary Magdalene's heart. So then what was it?

Rather than be drawn into aimless conjecture, Alex and Isa decided to enjoy the beauty of Thomas's quaint little town. Although it was late, there were still many people around.

They ambled up the broad stoned laneways and down the rough cobbled alleys. They passed newfangled storefronts with the latest of fashions set below timeworn apartments painted in the softest pastels. It seemed the kind of place Walt Disney might have come to seek inspiration.

They strolled through the park and caught sight of Thomas's fountain, still drizzling olive-drops from its leaves.

"We're back where we began," said Isa, when they stood once again in front of the beautiful bronze tree.

"Full circle," said Alex.

"Why did Thomas sculpt this fountain?"

"*Why?* I don't know, The statues he made for the town were an endowment to the island. For the sake of art, I suppose," said Alex. "But I'd venture to say he had other motives."

"All part of his elaborate puzzle," said Isa. "But how does this one fit in?"

"Your guess is as good as mine."

"A decoy for the undiscerning eye?" said Isa.

"We were fooled."

"*You* were fooled. Not me!" she laughed.

The soft lights in the park cast the sculpture in a spectacular glow. It was in front of this magnificent landscape of glistening bronze that the whole world disappeared before Alex's eyes. All that remained was the angel-like image of a beautiful, radiant star. Her name was Isabelle. Alex stood mesmerized by the depth of her beauty, the miracle that shined in her eyes.

Suddenly the loud pop of what could have only been a car's backfire interrupted their peace. Isa jumped. But before composure could set in, she jumped again. She pointed her arm over Alex's shoulder.

"Oh! Oh! Oh!"

Alex turned and followed Isa's finger. Not far from where they stood he could make out a brilliant bronze statue of Apollo.

"That's Thomas's too!" declared Isa, no question intended.

Alex could see that Isa was not all there, as if the greater part of her was floating mere inches off the ground. He knew better than to say or do anything to break the spell she was under.

Suddenly, words erupted from her lips. But they came out so fast, even she could hear that they formed only a jumble. She inhaled deeply and calmed down her tongue.

"This island!" she repeated. "La Maddalena! What does it mean?"

Alex's jaw dropped as he picked up her drift. *The heart of the Magdalene bears the light of this world.*

"We're in the heart of La Maddalena!" he gasped.

"And Thomas's statue?" she asked, staring at the beautiful bronze depiction of Apollo.

"He called it, Apollo In Gloria."

Isa nodded. "There in Apollo's chariot. What do you see?"

"The sun," said Alex.

"The light of this world!"

CHAPTER 83

*Y*ael sat inside a bland car that faded in with the others parked just up the street from the action. She watched as her two marks set to work on a bronze statue.

At first, she couldn't believe what she was looking at. It was the statue of the horse and chariot she'd once seen with the children that —later with Thomas—had become Pegasus.

She now saw what she hadn't before. The statue was identical to the stamp she'd studied so closely on the ransom envelope. Amedea Saroni's painting of Apollo In Gloria.

Strange that she hadn't made the connection before. How often we miss what's right before our faces. She wondered if it would have made a difference had she recognized it any sooner.

Things were now becoming clear. The masterminds of the heist, Niccolo and Thomas, had layered their escapade with a mythos of symbols. Whether they'd done this for their own amusement or with some greater purpose wasn't so clear. But it was evident that the images had been seeded from the very start of this all.

The first was the names. Niccolo San Tommaso. Thomas Esti. And the seal of St. Thomas. All three were Thomases. Yael was sure in this moment that each had been contrived. The janitor cum master-thief would have been using an alias, so too the boy-thief.

Next was the recurring theme of the archer. The seal of St. Thomas on the envelopes depicted the apostle carrying arrows on his back. So too the statue of St. Thomas at Thomas's home. As well as the statue of Apollo that her two marks were studying at this very moment — a full quiver of arrows was slung on his shoulder. Yael didn't even need to look to know that she'd find the very same image in Apollo In Gloria.

A quick internet search had confirmed the obvious. In addition to being the Sun God, Apollo was the Greek God of Archery. Hadn't San Tommaso and Thomas deployed their skill in archery to deliver the ransom exchange instructions into the Vatican Gardens?

Yael shook her head at the thought of how many-layered their scheme had been. It was a safe bet there'd be other nuances she had yet to pick out.

Following the crash that killed Thomas, Yael had waited at his house knowing that eventually, the desperate voice on the other end of Thomas's cellphone—*Alesi*, she presumed—would have to appear. She'd hoped more than known, but what real choice had she had?

While she'd waited, Yael scoured through the house looking for anything that might reveal the whereabouts of the Codex and Globe. It became quickly obvious and painfully so that Thomas had made them impossible to find. Better to wait for someone to come. It was just a matter of time.

She turned on the TV that night. The DVD came on automatically to show the trailing credits of an episode of *Columbo*. She restarted the show, stretched out on the sofa, and watched. She had a vague memory of the eccentric police detective and his quirky methods from the Seventies television series. She must have watched through the staircase banister while her fosters snored on the sofa.

This particular episode was about a misogynistic artist who cohabited with three generations of his lovers. The crime being investigated was the death of his oldest wife. But the complex twists and turns revealed a much older crime. The murder of a monocled and mustached art dealer named Harry Chudnow.

Yael's blood had boiled anew as the origin-story for Thomas's deceptions played out on the screen. Yael had let her guard down. She'd compromised on what she'd learned as a youth — the only way to be safe was to be in control, to be as the Perfect Warrior. She'd forgotten this, and it had cost her dearly, She'd never do so again. Never again.

And then it had happened. Her patience paid off. There'd been some movement as a sleek boat she spied in the night had slinked close to the shore.

Yael lurked in the shadows as two people climbed up from the sea. They veered off to the grove of pine trees and the cause of Yael's first trip to this island — the bronze statue of St. Thomas.

She came down the hill above the grove as near as she could without risk of being noticed and watched them fumble about for a time while they toyed with some things around their necks. It was too dark for Yael to make out what they were until they'd been inserted one by into a slot on the statue. Keys.

Yael almost pounced when a hidden compartment was opened — only to realize that all they'd retrieved was a small piece of canvas.

Not the Codex. Not the Bronze Globe.

She craned her head in order to hear what was said. *Clues.*

So this was a treasure hunt. And they were following breadcrumbs left behind by Thomas.

As tempting as it had been for Yael to rush them then and there and abscond with their satchel of clues, she knew it would have been a risky move.

It was risky to presume that the directions Thomas had left weren't personal in nature, clues that could only be deciphered by Alesi and the woman he was with.

CHAPTER 84

*Y*ael now sat inside a silver Alfa Romeo she'd stolen from a vacant house on the isle. She'd been able to tell by the white sheets on the furniture that the owners weren't there, likely in their principal home in Rome or Zurich or further away.

So she'd plucked the car from the garage and later swapped the plates with those from a similar car she'd found on the big island of Sardinia. Private Dick-ery 101.

The Alfa's GPS system had served her well in tailing her marks around the island while they'd followed the clues. She'd been able to stay back in the distance and anticipate their moves based on the map displayed on the screen. A tracker-signal would have been perfect, but she hadn't anticipated the need — and using her sleuthing skills made for a more suspenseful chase.

She hadn't been able to see what they'd found at the tree-fountain in town, but then she'd followed them to the middle of nowhere where they'd pulled a crystalline block from beneath a huge olive tree. The word *Codex* had echoed through the trees.

Yael was thrilled. The quest of this knight and his maiden was to gather the Treasure. Yael now knew she need only continue her pursuit and at the right moment step forth and claim it as her own.

As she sat hunched in the Alfa, she was tasting the anticipation roll on her tongue while her two marks, brilliant sleuths in their own right, worked on Apollo. Before long, they managed to unlock the Sun in its celestial chariot. It came apart like a matryoshka revealing its child. It was hard to see clearly from this distance, but Yael could imagine the son of the Sun sitting there in its throne, Mary Magdalene's Sacred Bronze Globe.

She watched as the man struggled to carry the heavy object into the back seat of the Range Rover. He held it in place while the woman strapped the seatbelt around it. Yael was nearly ready for checkmate. She'd follow them one last time to be sure there wasn't something else yet to be found.

Yael tailed them as they drove back to the north. She kept her lights off, left a healthy distance and trusted both the map on the screen and her own sharp instincts to guide her through the dark.

They didn't appear to be driving in the direction of Thomas's house and their speedboat. Nor to any of the ferries. It seemed that they were heading back to the old olive tree in the heart of the island where the glass block had been found.

Had they discovered another clue?

Yael held her eyes on the Range Rover's taillights until they disappeared over a hilltop ahead on the road. She wasn't worried since the GPS showed a straightaway, and so she crept slowly up the hill, careful to maintain the same distance. No need to spook them before they dug up the rest.

As Yael reached the top of the hill she was surprised to find no taillights in sight. She'd have expected to see them up ahead if they'd been driving back to the olive tree. Clearly, they weren't.

Yael turned to the GPS. At the speed they'd been traveling, the only place they could have gone in such a short time would have been onto the first of the three roads ahead.

She turned right onto the narrow lane and drove slowly. After a couple of minutes, she came to a dead-end and turned back to the main road. Could they have made it to the second turnoff before she'd crested the hill?

As Yael began her turn left onto the second lane, the Range Rover appeared as if out of nowhere on the side of the road ahead. Yael stopped mid-turn and realized too late that doing so had flushed her out.

There was a momentary stalemate before the Range Rover suddenly jumped onto the road heading north away from Yael, churning the dirt on the road's edge and accelerating fast.

The chase was on!

Yael stepped on the gas, flicked on the high beams and pursued. The pair had the more powerful car and enough of a head start, but the Alfa was no slouch and Yael was sure that she was the better driver. She might not make up much of the distance between them, but she'd have them when they slowed down, which they'd eventually have to do on an island this small.

Their speeds continued to climb as Yael tailed them onto the coastal road. They had a good lead, and she briefly lost them when they rounded a turn.

The memory of her fateful chase a few days ago flashed through her mind. This would end differently.

Another hairpin curve and she lost sight again. Suddenly, above the barreling of the Alfa's motor, she heard the screeching of tires. She came around the bend and caught the tail end of disaster.

Yael slammed on her brakes and watched helplessly as the Range Rover flew off the road skyward before bombing down to the sea.

Yael brought her car to a loud skid-mark stop and ran to the edge of the cliff.

There was not a damn thing she could do but watch as the Range Rover let go its last gasp and slid beneath the churning sea.

CHAPTER 85

Yael tottered on the edge of the cliff. She peered out where the Range Rover had plunged with the Treasure inside. Sunk beneath the black ink of night. None but the sea would survive.

She stood there in disbelief. And at that very moment there on the small rocky outcrop hovering over the cold waters of the Mediterranean a huge wave of emotions rolled in. It pummeled her as she realized where exactly she stood.

What had just happened? She was in the very same spot that mere days before she'd come across the bloody corpse of Thomas in front of his mangled car.

The clouds seemed to have gathered in obeisance, darkening the sky and the water and the air in between.

Yael stood there alone feeling nothing but pain. It began in her knees and spread out from there. But it was not the pain of the wild kick from Thomas. Not even the pelting of stones from the Aston. It was not *that* pain she felt.

It was a penetrating ache deep in her bones that pummeled her to the core. She knew not from where it did come. But pain it was, absolute and profound.

Sweat erupted all over her skin. Her tears poured. Her chest ached. Anguish coursed like hot oil through her veins. Yael bunched up her fists as a rage erupted from her bowels. She could not truly know from what depths it arose. But rise it did, and she could contain it no more.

Her anger rolled free, and she let loose a feral scream that had been building ever since that fateful day on the balcony.

And in that moment Yael was transported to the little girl peering out through the crack in the doorway. Watching in shock as her mother threw herself against the very spot she'd warned Yael to be careful of so many times before.

Hearing the shriek. Just one. Cut short. Like all air had been stripped from her mother mid-scream as she tumbled headfirst from their top floor balcony.

Fear squeezed Yael's heart, a corset's laces pulled tight and refusing to break.

And for the first time, the memory was different. It didn't end with her eyes glued to the railing as she waited in fright for her mother's return.

"Mama!" the little girl screamed and bolted to the spot, leaping onto the old wooden milk crate.

"Mama, where are you?!"

The little girl always climbed onto the paint-flecked milk crate to drop orange feathers in the wind. The top floor of the mansion was where they lived. It was their own special penthouse apartment. The rest of the house beneath them was spooky — curtains always drawn, sheets over sofas, and musty.

The balcony wound around three sides of the apartment. And with birds aplenty where they lived, this gave her lots of space to hunt for her feathers. She dipped the white ones in food coloring. Orange worked best to follow their journey. Then she dropped them over the rail and watch as they floated in the sky. She even fashioned binoculars out of toilet paper rolls to hold the feathers in her sights as long as she could. The best feathers were the ones that would fall in a gentle arc, spinning their way down in much the same way as her bubble bath would twirl down into the drain.

Mama, where are you?

She pulled the last of the day's feathers from her pocket and dropped it. She lifted herself high on her toes on the milk crate, higher than she imagined she could.

But it wasn't high enough. So the little girl with the tiny fingers gripped the railing and hoisted her chest onto the top rail. She teetered and tottered as she peered through the night. A couple of people were fussing over something on the ground.

Had they found her orange feather?

The little girl with the tiny fingers lifted the binoculars to her face. That's when she caught sight of the pretty pattern of Mama's blue and white dress. It was disappearing fast, a deep shock of red spreading in its place.

In a dreamlike moment, the little girl spotted orange circling its way through the sky. *If only...* She leaned out her hands as far as she could trying to reach for her feather.

"*WHY?!*" Yael cried out to the sea.

That very instant, a strong wind responded, quite out of the blue, throwing her back on her heels. She looked up at the sky as if to receive a sign. Her arms were spread wide. Her hair and clothes fluttered wildly as they clung to her skin.

The fury was quickening when, without warning, the powerful gust abruptly stopped.

It warped Yael's sense of balance. The same muscles that had just held her upright against the in-blowing wind were now rocking her forward in the instant of its absence.

Yael was flung ahead into the space where the granite edge ended.

Where the magnets of the froth-laden rock took hold from below.

The little girl was tumbling now, her orange feather long gone.

In its stead, the angry waters of Maddalena's rocky shore rushed up to meet her.

CHAPTER 86

The dashing young lad stepped into the flower shop, his brow heavy with sadness. A coarse silver cross hung low on his chest.

"Bongiorno," the joyful petal peddler said. "Your mermaid still sleeps?"

The boy's dark eyes held the answer in silence as he plucked the prettiest bouquet. He dropped some coins in the old man's hand, crossed the street and climbed to the third floor of the small island hospital.

He looked hopefully to the two nurses seated at their station. One smiled tightly back. Nothing had changed. He walked past the lone woman seated in the small alcove on his way to the room at the end of the hall.

Once he'd gone, the younger of the two nurses twirled her hair on a finger and spun around on her stool.

"Tell me a story!" she said playfully. "Who is that?"

"Handsome, isn't he?" They spoke in their own Maddalenino tongue.

"Gorgeous. *And so tall!*"

"He comes every day to see our Sleeping Beauty."

"Every day?"

"For weeks now."

"How have I missed seeing him?"

The woman in the alcove didn't seem bothered by the chatter at the front. From what the nurses could tell, she was in her own world, either in mourning or preparing to be.

"Well now, sit still," the older nurse said. "Here's a story for you. He caught our Sleeping Beauty."

"Really?" the young one said with googly eyes.

"He's a fisherman. Had been at sea when a storm came in. Was returning to shore when he saw a car go over the cliff. Remember that fuss with all the divers in the north?"

"He saw that happen?" she asked incredulously.

"Yes. Well, it sank before he could do anything. But then he heard a voice cry out in the storm. Saw Sleeping Beauty standing at the cliff's edge where the car had gone over. Through the rain, he heard her yell but could not make out her words. Only the screams. And before he knew it, she too had fallen into the sea."

"She jumped?"

The tired nurse shrugged.

"He rescued her?"

"Yes."

"How romantic."

"And now he comes every day with fresh flowers and sits by her bed."

"Her prince," the young nurse sighed and spun again on her stool. She twirled her hair tightly as if to make ringlets.

"What's his name?"

"They call him Tritone."

The two nurses didn't notice when the woman in the alcove rose from her seat and slipped from the ward. She was dressed completely in black. Dark sunglasses and a wide-brimmed hat cast shadows over her face. A trace of vanilla swirled in the air.

Only one thing stood out. Lips dipped in the reddest of paint, properly shaped to a succulent yet saucy pout.

EPILOGUE

MEIGGA

|\/| ONE |\/|

It was the midpoint of night. When the light of day circled furthest away. When heaven's torches twinkled their brightest.

A beautiful girl looked up to the sky in wonderment. Her name was Meigga, and she was child-like, though not a child. She'd been playing, though not playing. Precise and purposeful in her actions. Meditative in her countenance.

The star on this night was Luna. And she was majestic in full glory overlooking a sacred spot somewhere in what some in faraway lands might know as the Valdivian rainforest of western Patagonia.

Meigga imagined that from Luna's throne high above, she could be seen playing alone on the moonlit sands of a beach.

Meigga wore a loose woolen cloth shaped like a poncho draped over her shoulders, a braided vine belt snug at her waist.

A resin-soaked torch cast flames at her side, while a plateau of smoothed sand set the perfect stage.

Petals of all colors had been set with wet sand to display a beautiful circular mandala of seemingly-random, intricate, hypnotic symbols.

At the center was a pyramid made of stones and seashells. At its base lay tightly-packed twigs, leaves and dried moss.

Meigga reached for her torch and touched the fire to her creation. The pyre magically came to life.

Luna would have noticed that at the very same moment, off in the distance, a pair of luminescent gold eyes flashed from the dunes. Their possessor's fur was dark, though not black, with markings much like an intricate sky-scape of shadowed constellations.

Meigga's gaze remained true to her ritual afire, much as Luna held true to the child in her sights. For the girl had sneaked away from her village to fulfill only one purpose. To celebrate the vital wonder of Luna in fullness.

Just as Luna herself did surely shine in awe at the magnificence of Meigga.

MEIGGA

|\/| TWO |\/|

Meigga sat entranced for some time in front of the fire. Her eyes danced with the flames as they rose and they fell, as they leaned one way and they leaned another.

Soon she stood, ever-fluid in her quiet movements, and slipped out of her dress, revealing her youthful womanhood to the heavens. She walked serenely to the water's edge. There she let the sea gently wash her feet before she leapt forward and dove headlong into the next cresting wave.

Meigga swam and splashed in the shallows — a trusting dolphin at play with the surf.

Luna held watch as the golden-eyed creature began his slink over rock and sand, creeping ever-slowly ever-closer to the prize he had spied. And then in a heartbeat, he took flight. In the short span of a few dozen strides, he halved the distance between himself and the girl.

Suddenly, as if out of nowhere, a colossal thunderclap boomed from the heavens. It came alone in darkness and cracked its mighty whip with a snap so sharp as to break the broadest of necks.

The black dappled jaguar was stunned to obeisance, frozen mid-pace.

In an instant, a strong wind swept up the drier sands of the dunes and created a swirling fog of dust and grit.

Luna watched in peace as the one with the golden eyes turned in retreat, ebbing away from the sea.

The waters now choppy, Meigga rose from the surf and ran to her fire. She touched her head to the sand as another great roll of thunder crescendoed and boomed. This time the earth beneath her shook, and Meigga's ritual tower of stones and shells fell apart.

Quickly, she set to her feet, pulled her dress over her head and took off in a sprint.

Through the building wisps of cloud, Luna could make out a curious grin spread wide on Meigga's face as she raced back home to her village.

MEIGGA

|\/| THREE |\/|

Another day had come.

The waters of what some distant ones might call the South Pacific crashed into the massive boulders at the base of the cliff throwing spray high into the air. Meigga watched in fascination from her perch in the shelter of a little cove as the spray hung for a moment before falling back to the sea. It reminded her what it had felt like to be thrown up in the sky by her father when she was still a child, that moment of hanging weightlessly before falling back in his arms.

Meigga looked over at her little brother, who glanced up to meet her gaze. She had played the same game with Huenchumir when he was just a baby. But he'd grown too big now for her to lift him in that way.

They had come out to the shore to gather clams for their supper. At her side was her catch, held in a pail made of tightly bound palm fronds and lined with long grass.

Meigga had collected enough and now sat on a large boulder jutting out from the cliff wall, quietly watching Huenchumir through the mist as he dutifully, almost meditatively, dug around the rocks and sand for the little mollusks.

She loved her brother like he was her very own son. The years that separated them had been enough to call forth a maternal instinct in her, all the same love and wonderment that a first child evokes.

Meigga had never really thought about it in this way. All she knew was that her love for him was transcendent. Glorious. And beautiful.

It was the kind of love that had no need to be seen. No need for appreciation. The experience alone, the feeling alone, was her greatest reward.

And she knew that Huenchumir was equally nourished by her, regardless of whether he was even aware of her devotions at one moment or another.

Meigga's attention was now captured by a movement at the top of the cove's opposite cliff. A pair of golden eyes flashed through the mist.

Her old friend was back.

MEIGGA

|\/| FOUR |\/|

Meigga had not seen golden-eyes before, but she had felt him. And his name became clear in the moment.

Yaga.

He was eyeing her as he stealthily carved a slow descent towards her down the rocky, muddy wall.

She could make out Yaga's near elephantine roars over the ocean's mighty percussion.

Meigga stood tall on the rock, then took one large bounding step forward and dove in a perfect arc the five lengths of her body to the waters below. The waves were higher than usual, but Meigga swam mostly just below the raucousness.

She came up only twice before she found herself in line with the innermost point of the cove, afloat like a freely-bobbing coconut at the midpoint between where she and Yaga had begun.

Huenchumir must have spied her and was now slowly making his way closer along the rocks.

Behind her, the skies had changed, with a wave of billowing grey clouds sweeping in from the deep.

Yaga was halfway down the cliff when Meigga spotted him again.

I've never seen a jaguar before, she thought. *You're not known in these parts.*

Yaga had been slinking closer and closer. He was now about ten-and-five of her lengths away, up and in to the land.

You're beautiful! she thought. *Look, Huenchumir!*

Meigga turned intuitively to her brother who too had drawn close.

The little boy turned to see where his big sister was pointing and shrieked at the sight of the ferocious jaguar lurking above.

Yaga roared.

Huenchumir dropped his pail. All of his clams spilled out at his feet. He stood quivering like he'd been frozen by the rains and winds of winter.

Huenchumir!

MEIGGA

|\/| FIVE |\/|

Like her brother, Meigga too was suddenly entrapped — in her case by the sudden shift in the wind and the tide which tossed her about like a dried tumble of weeds swept up in desert sands.

The midday sky was disappearing, cast darker by the rolling grays above her.

Suddenly, a rippling flash filled the sky. The thunder-blast that followed penetrated the very water Meigga swam in and punched a pulse of energy through her body.

A barrage of lightning and thunder followed that spun day into night into day into night.

On the rocks, Yaga's roars had grown more and more insistent. Meigga turned to the dazzling gold orbs that penetrated her blues.

Run! said his voice through her mind. *Run home now!*

She could feel a quickening force deep within the ocean cresting intensely.

Meigga kicked herself high in the air like a dolphin. She drew in a huge breath then sunk beneath the roil of the surf and swam in to shore. There she bounded to her frightened boy, took his chin in her hand and looked deeply into his eyes till he blinked.

Huenchumir!

She gripped his hand firmly and guided him forward. Together they leapt from one stone to the next, climbing ever higher up the cliff.

As the wall grew steeper, Huenchumir took the lead. He climbed like none other, fingers and toes instinctively nesting in the least visible of nooks and propelling him upward. Meigga had only to follow his path.

Yaga took chase, though his clumsy paws scrambled and slipped on the loosened mud and water-drenched stones.

Behind them, in the closing distance of the ocean's expanse, a tremendous force could be seen barreling toward Meigga's cove.

A great wave had arisen.

And it powerfully tumbled and grew.

MEIGGA

|\/| SIX |\/|

It was after the passage of some suns and moons since the great wave had washed clean their land that Huenchumir could be found peeking over the very top of a grassy hillside.

It was the stillness of night. And he'd snuck only just high enough to see Meigga through a squint of his eyes bouncing in the distance as she swept across the verdant starlit plain.

If there had been more light on this New Moon night, or if he had raised his head only slightly, he would have captured the scene full in its splendor.

Meigga atop the black jaguar, her knees clenched tightly as she gripped the patchwork fur in her fists. A ring made of flowers and vine tight around her head.

Far beyond the span of sight, from what could only be described as the outer edges of an amorphous sphere, a second massive shock wave suddenly erupted.

The pulse barreled inward like an invisible shooting star, moving toward them from the furthest edges of the Universe.

It moved rapidly into the Milky Way in the direction of Earth, to the indiscernible Patagonia-at-night.

A flash emerged from the heavens with the impossible thunder crack of cosmic dimensions.

The strike came down like a mighty arrow and touched the very tip of Meigga's crown.

Meigga and Yaga were bathed in the light.

A curious grin spread wide on her face.

Run! Meigga shouted.

Black Yaga, Run!

ABOUT THE AUTHOR

Shams-Tabriz is a consummate entrepreneur. He resides in Vancouver and reclines in Bali — and wherever else his good heart desires.

Look for **THE MAGDALENE PROPHECY** trilogy on Amazon.
QUICKENING Book One
TREASURE HUNT Book Two
STYX & STONES Book Three (Summer 2020)

Shams-Tabriz is also the author of
SOARING WITH ANGELS
A personal account on his spiritual journey.

Visit the author at
www.shams-tabriz.com
Instagram & FaceBook: @ShamsTabrizStoryteller

Made in the USA
Middletown, DE
05 July 2021